The Stone-Mas
(Lightning in the Wyntr)

BK 1
-
Gemma

Copyright © 2020 by RJ Vlier

All rights reserved. This book or any portion thereof may not be reproduced or transmitted in any form or manner, electronic or mechanical, including photocopying, recording, or by any information storage or retrieval system, without the express written permission of the copyright owner except for the use of brief quotations in a book review or other noncommercial uses permitted by copyright law.

Mail to: rjvlier@rjvlier.com_
This publication is also available online at: www.rjvlier.com
Copyright © 2020 by RJ Vlier Books

Printed in the United States of America

Library of Congress Control Number:	2020912114
ISBN: Softcover	978-1-64908-033-2
eBook	978-1-64908-032-5

Republished by: PageTurner Press and Media LLC
Publication Date: 07/22/2020

To order copies of this book, contact:

PageTurner Press and Media
Phone: 1-888-447-9651
order@pageturner.us
www.pageturner.us

DEDICATION:

For those who have loved to read short stories with an ending. This is for you, the one that wants something different and out of the ordinary. I enjoyed writing this and hope that you get a little 'something' out of it, I know that I did!

This goes out to those that have gone through personal traumas and also physical ones.

Working on this during the time of May 2020 flooding in Sanford, MI. The town where I went to school was devastated when two upper dams released. Actually one failed major as the berm collapsed, sending Wixom Lake downstream like a tsunami. The upper Sanford Lake filled quickly, flooding areas taking roads, bridges and aiming for the Sanford Dam. The water did get around it and tore through the village.

Just before this all we had nearly 24 hours of rain hitting the upper middle of Michigan. These waters did what they normally do, head south. This then hit Wixom Lake and flooded lower areas there, but the water kept coming and pounding against the two dams. One levy broke and sent it all down stream.

This year is also the 150th year for Sanford. It was designated "Village" in the late 70's but to me, it is still home. The good news is that not one life was lost. Property, homes, so many things. But many things can be replaced.

Sad. Heartbreaking.

DISCLAIMER:

Neither the author nor the publisher shall be held liable or responsible to any person or entity with respect to any loss or incidental or consequential damages caused, or alleged to have been caused, directly or indirectly, by the information or programs contained herein. No warranty may be created or extended by sales representatives or written sales materials. Every company is different and the advice and strategies contained herein may not be suitable for your situation

Thank you to those that assist me. By simply reading, the book checks for corrections or just to follow me and smile for support. I want you to know that I appreciate you more than I can say.
I know who you are and I tell them constantly. Verbal. I like it that way.
MaryKay who drops everything to read for me.
Another who finds (and places) commas for fun.
And others that love to read and give me feedback.

I write to create an illusion.
Wanting you to go to another world by opening a page, by reading a line even if it is just for a small period of time.
I write to tell a story. As my father was, I also am a storyteller. I only do it by writing, not as one to sit and tell a story out loud to others.

Thank you for following me.
Thank you for reading my work.
Thank you for being there with me for this short time as you read.

I appreciate you all,

RJ Vlier

Table of Contents:

Prologue .... *xi*
Chapter 1 .... *1*
Chapter 2 .... *5*
Chapter 3 .... *7*
Chapter 4 .... *13*
Chapter 5 .... *19*
Chapter 6 .... *23*
Chapter 7 .... *29*
Chapter 8 .... *37*
Chapter 9 .... *41*
Chapter 10 .... *49*
Chapter 11 .... *53*
Chapter 12 .... *65*
Chapter 13 .... *73*
Chapter 14 .... *79*
Chapter 15 .... *83*
Chapter 16 .... *87*
Chapter 17 .... *101*
Chapter 18 .... *111*
Chapter 19 .... *127*
Chapter 20 .... *137*
Chapter 21 .... *145*
Chapter 22 .... *157*
Chapter 23 .... *165*
Chapter 24 .... *177*
Chapter 25 .... *183*
Chapter 26 .... *193*
Epilogue *201*

Book intro

Solving a mystery was NOT on the agenda for today. Also it was NOT just another morning. Sunday. Feb. Super Bowl sunday morning and 2AM?
　　　Nope. Not on my agenda. But, here we are.
The stories of family, the memories of some and more from another. To tell of family or to tell of the old country. We are Scottish, we tell stories.
　　　Stories of old, some newer as to being here in the New Land.
　　　This and so much more was passed generation to generation.
　　　Today it again gets passed along but without the knowledge of one.

　　　<u>One</u> *that causes change. Change to the life, change to the heart and change to what will be. The story of the huge rock named The Stone-Mas.*
　　　Gemma McWyntr lives for her ranch. It is small in comparison to those around her as she raises Brahma's there is no need to have 100 or more acres. The ranch is nestled in between a large wooded area and the mountains . Protected by wind and bad weather.
　　　This family who lived here for generations only had one child each. A male who carried the name, now, Gemma as an only child and knew that the family name would die with her.
　　　Gemma joked and said she would find a guy willing to take the family name. Her mother would shake her head and laugh.

The storm came. The wind. The change that affected everything and everyone. Where Gemma was once alone, now she had several men who appeared. Did the stone bring them here?

Prologue

Denton, MT. A small town of 301 after the Census of 2000. A place where everyone knows everyone and if you don't, then you weren't born here. A good thing or a bad thing depending on who you are having a conversation with at the time.

My name is Gemma, Geraldine McWyntr I live several miles north of town on a 60 acre ranch. Small by standards of the other ranches nearby. I have lived here alone now for the last two years since Pop passed away. Our place consists of more forest than open land. You can see mountains, trees, and my babies, Brahmas.

The land is open for them to get out of the barn and stretch their legs, chase each other and play with the babies. Pop raised them for years. You may have seen them in and around rodeos. Pulling wagons and such. Not everyone has a longhorn. I sell more to Canadians than here. But that could be because I am this far north.

But I found out something one day when a friend of Pop was over. He did rodeos and had ridden a bull or two. And now, I have two brahmas that I travel with that are really good at bucking guys off.

But at nearly two tons each of fun for a bull rider. Yes, I rent my babies out for sport. And I first started when a rodeo friend, Nick, had visited. He took one look at my bull and said that he would make a great ride. I, of course, laughed but saw that he was serious.

I moved to Come-N-GetMe (because when he was a babe just over a year old) I had to chase him to get him inside. Well, I talked to my bull and saw how he looked back at the guy and then me and actually nodded his head. I swore, he-nodded-his -head! Like he wanted to do this!

So, I let Nick get a ride. Nick just happened to have his gear with him in the truck. We got him all set-up beside the fence in the corral. Pop told him to *do good or go home*. I laughed and then did my best to be serious.

I held Come-N-GetMe's head, Pop had leaned over the side of the fence, we looked at Nick then let him go when Nick nodded.

Annnnd my bull tossed him like a wet noodle. 2, possibly 3 second ride. Nick said *it was a trial*. Then we did it all again and again.

Every - single - time Come-N-GetMe tossed his fine ass into the air.

Nick gave us a name, Pop made some calls and me and my bull went to a rodeo for a job interview.

I gasped and yelled seeing the cowboys in spurs and acting as they did. I remember apologizing like crazy as I walked my guy back to the trailer. I was upset. Not with him or his performance, no. But at the treatment.

But I had not made it very far when I was stopped by a manager who said my bull needed to go back. Because his name was drawn for the 2nd round and that he was a *hell of a bull*, we went back. No one rode him for more than 4 seconds. And Come-N-GetMe did not seem bothered.

OK, when he was held in that tight box, he snorted and pawed. And when they opened the gate he dumped the rider and stood looking around at everyone like it was a game.

I was not allowed inside the ring to retrieve him but told the rider who went out to be nice. He laughed, tipped his hat and said, 'yes ma'am.'

So, the guys get to 'play rodeo' and I have a side income. My bulls get exercise and some time away from the ranch.

Come back and play nice with the ladies. I noticed they haven't complained yet.

They get their 'battle' scars and I worry. But all in all, the ranch is doing quite well.

But, there is more to this story……..

#1 is that Pop passed away.
Sudden.
And I am here.
Alone.

*Damn realtor jerks showed up the day **after** his funeral. Must be those guys that live reading the obits....*
There is a consortium. This group loves to buy up ranches. They stroll into town, talk big to everyone and toss money around as they get the small ranches. Turn them around and have breeding farms. Huge places that have cattle that never step foot out of the barns. They breed, calve, give milk and repeat.
Don't have use for a bull because they buy the semen.
Kinda sad.
Not a life.
And we, dedicated ranchers have ignored their asses.
Stayed away from them and so far, kept them out of our county. Protecting it. If a ranch is here it is family owned and ran. If the owner sells, a neighbor will purchase. Thus keeping the consortium out and away.
Until today.

Here I am, still reeling from Pop being gone, the funeral and now this? The time spent in the hospital, talking to doctors. Finding decent food to keep myself going. Staying beside the man who raised me.
Taught me to do what was needed. Gave me a shoulder to lean on especially after mom passed. I learned to handle the ranch. Learned to handle the house. Handled things that mom did. Kept the gardens, both of them. Flowers and vegetables and herbs.
Sitting beside his bed.
Talked to him when he was lucid and held his hand when he slept.
Watched as he got weaker and weaker.

Then the funeral. Talking with friends and feeling lost. Food that was brought over. So many sat and ate or stood around and talked. We reminisce and memories flowed.

I still feel lost. My friends and Mom and Pop's friends left. I got up and did normal morning things then at 10AM
I got pissed off.
I got some target practice.
They asked for it.
This is a working ranch and everyone knows that ranchers don't back down and, most important, ranchers know how to handle a gun or rifle.
Varmints come in all sizes. And not all of them have four legs.

Well, I did ask nicely for them to get the hell off my property, my *private* property, as I stood there in my work clothes. Jeans, t-shirt with a long flannel over it. It was Pops flannel as I was still feeling blue when I got up.
Me, standing there because when I heard the cars and did not recognize them as one of my many neighbors possibly coming over to give their condolences. I stepped out onto the wide wrap-around porch and, due to habit, grabbed Pops rifle on my way out the door.
Habit. Something instilled into me from living here. As Pop would have done, I acted normal and protected what was mine. I would do it again and again if it would keep *them* away.

I knew what was in the will. I was there when the lawyer was here at the ranch. Mom and Pop had things all set up and I would be the proud owner of the ranch. No stipulations.
And the place is paid for and there are no liens on it. Just me and the animals now. Both safe and secure……

I did not expect to lose them. My parents. It is not something that you even talk about.
I love this place and will keep it but - I had not thought that I would have to *fight* for it within 24 hours of the funeral.

When one old fart snickered, I racked and filled his grill full of buckshot. In a way I hoped it was a loaner car, he would have to explain the damage. I felt good as I racked the rifle again and aimed for another's tires and said loud enough for them both to hear, "I could just let a bull lose and save my ammo you know."

This is when they looked and saw what exactly was on this ranch and now was watching them. Not a horse or a cow. A full grown Brahma bull. One that was now snorting and pawing the ground.

Guess someone did not do their homework.

My Brahma's, babies all of them, (well to me.) They are gentle unless provoked. Or if there is a cowboy on their back. And needless to say strangers bug them and strangers that I shot at? Ya, the big guys are **very interested.**

I have seen them run off a wolf that was after a youngster And, I have seen them in the ring. To face a brahma takes a strong person.

If you step outside the house they look, if you get off the porch, they get curious and will mosey over. Maybe even bellow.

For attention. For a head scratch. For nearly anything. Because around me and my friends who visit, they are calm. They know how to get out, just go back through the barn and out their personal 'doggie' door.

But the two men did not know that. And after hearing the rifle blast, the bulls became more than curious.

When a big head followed by shoulders came out from the front of the barn.... Followed by another. Moving and swinging their huge heads around....

Tossing a head into the air and a bellow.....

The guy then dove into his car and they both left in a cloud of dust. I sat down on the steps, not to laugh or cry. Just from exhaustion. The whole thing was hitting me. Crashing down, knowing the only males were these guys to take care of me now.

I put Pop's rifle across my legs and looked out over what is now my spread. I looked up at Cotton Candy who was the closest, watched the taillights disappear then he looked at me. Guessing that I was fine, he turned and went back inside followed by Goose-Eg who is a year younger.

I sat there and tears ran down my face. This was sudden. Too soon. Finding feelings that I had held back for some time now being released.

I have 10 Brama's total with a few males, one age 4 the others age 2 and one age 1 but just as large.

I don't 'farm' them all out. Just this year it was two at a time. The others are babies yet. And hell, not all Brahmas want to buck men off their backs. Some are so gentle....

This pays for shots and other vet bills. Have hay and grain for their food and other supplies. Actually, the ranch runs itself. Not like I have to mow the back acres. Just a section here in the front.

Take care of the flowers grandma and mom planted. Tend the garden, you know, regular things. Not every waking moment is with the animals. And Pop taught me the books and records. That is mainly in the office part.

I sit up and look around, wipe my face.

I think that the 'guys' talk and hey, if they like the travel and the challenge, I don't care. And my big guys have shoved several more at me. I just may have four more on the circuit to run with them. But only if they want to.

OK, the bulls talk to each other. Seriously. My guys do.

It was to be a good year Pop said when we went over the accounts last month. Everything balanced out. The good vs the bad. The only bad thing is the weather. Spring moving in late so I won't get the garden in around the usual time. Will have to tinker with the tiller. Or just get a new one. They don't last forever.

I get to see nature at her finest up here away from unnatural lights that come from the city. Talk of the Northern Lights? I get a great view. Sit on the back of the porch, see the colors pop around the mountains. See the slow movement. Gets mesmerizing and then you feel your ass freezing and snap out of it to go inside.

I have trees to watch get green, sway in a summer breeze. Change of the colors to rich reds and golds as I ride my horse around the back section. The pines are nice for windbreaks, but the others for color, can't beat it.

Yes. I love it here. I love the quiet and I even love taking care of the Brahmas. The adorable babies with their floppy ears and ….

I swallow. Tears flow again.

Doc said it was only the flu.

Then Pop couldn't breathe.

The clinic said pneumonia.

They took him by ambulance, I followed in the truck to the hospital so I knew exactly where he was.

And he never recovered.

It was fast and …

I was suddenly … alone.

I was not supposed to turn 25 alone.

This was a year that I had looked forward to. Not that there was a guy in the picture. But. We had made plans and now, I look up at the sky then at the barns.

No boyfriends, no babies, nothing. Being single sucks big time. I could really use a hug right now.

Tears rolled down my face and nearly froze, it was damn cold for April but hey, I'm not complaining. Here it is high up and I love it for that. My ass was on the porch, booted feet on the steps and there I sat for nearly an hour.

I had just sent people, absolute strangers off my ranch with a loaded rifle. I would not be surprised that the next vehicle is a police car. Though the sheriff is a friend, if a complaint was made....

My life was not supposed to be like this.

But this place is my home and here I will stay.

Chapter 1

My last date had been to my Senior Prom. Excited? Hell yes. Dwayne Mitchell was older. Had signed up to work at the ranch next door. Met him when a friend (my BFF) got me talked into a blind date.
OK, I met him so it was not exactly a 'blind date'. The guy was an unknown to me so Pop said I had to meet him.

Freddie, Frederica was my bestie since the 2nd grade. Dwayne started working at her parents ranch. She called, I visited, met the guy and things were nice between us.

Things went well, Freddie mentioned the prom and our dates (her boyfriend at the time and Dwayne) talked since her new boyfriend was also working for her dad.

Mom and I shopped for a dress. I even got the tickets, not like the guy could just stop at the school and get them. And no, I am NOT the person that takes control. Hell, I was there so no problem.

I have my own income from my work. Pop pays well and I save it as I don't have many things I need to spend money on. OK, a decent pair of cowboy boots. We girls need our *things*.

I made a point to stop at the ranch while he worked and give him the tickets so he would be the one to hand them over when we arrived. You know, a guy thing. He smiled, gave me a kiss on the cheek and I left. I turned, walking backwards to my truck, and mentioned that the flowers would be ready also and named the shop I ordered from.

He laughed and said, "I got it babe." He held the tickets up.

I smiled and waved back, got in my truck and left. He called me babe. I smiled all the way home.

That night I got dressed and waited. I had found a rather great dress. Mom said it was 'princess length' as it was just past my knees. The neckline was covered with sparkles and I wore mom's necklace for a treat.

My arms were bare but the top had wide straps, well wide material that covered my shoulders. The colors started light, then gradually went darker to a deep rose. I remember twirling for Mom and Pops after coming down the stairs.

Mom took a few pictures and we waited for Dwayne to take more.

The weather was nice and I was nervous as I waited. Watching out the window and wondered if he had a truck or a car. Not that it mattered but all these thoughts ran through my head.

We were to meet up with others and eat dinner. Dwayne was to pick me up around 6PM and I was ready, sitting with mom and nervous as hell. My leg bouncing from either nerves or excitement. Mom said that I would wrinkle the dress. I remembered just shaking my head because I would be sitting in a car, then sitting at the restaurant.

I sat there at the table looking out the window, waiting and my phone buzzed vibrating across the surface, Freddie was texting me, "Where are you? And why is Dwayne here with Pricilla?"

I felt it in my gut. No. No-no-no.....

Then Ben texted, followed by Scott then Tyler. My besties who I knew since school and junior and senior high. Everyone who I was to have dinner with.

Well, I saw red!

I **gave** <u>him</u> the tickets as a gesture. So others would assume he paid for them. I talked about our dinner plans, the reservations and….

I looked at my phone. Pictures now came across the face.

Pics of the two of them at dinner.

The dinner I was supposed to be at.

I stood and checked my clutch for the receipt for the tickets - a backup in case he lost them. I remember that I said something like *'wires got crossed, I am meeting him there.'* Mom and Pop looked at me. Did they know? I did not say anything before running out the door.

I jumped into my truck, being careful with my dress, and took off for the KC Building that our Senior group had decorated this week.

Getting out, I slammed the truck door then winced. No need to take it out on old Benjamin. (It costs several Benjamin's to keep gas in him, hence the name). Making my way inside, I nodded to friends and their dates as I passed. I made it down a hall or two. Could hear the music playing and laughter.

Stepping up to the table I looked at old Ms. Bremer. She smiled as she looked up at me, "Ticket please. You look nice tonight dear." As I said, small town. Everyone knows everyone and now everyone will know this.

My embarrassment.

She looked around me as if I was hiding someone.

I gave her a huge smile, "I ran late, we were meeting here." (Fake it until you make it.) I slid the receipt over that had the numbers on it and she checked her list, looked up, "Are you sure hon?"

She could see that the numbers for my tickets were marked off in her records just the same as I could standing there, looking down at the list. She frowned.

I was about to answer when I looked up and saw Dwayne and Pricilla glide pass the doorway, dancing by during a slow number. I fisted both hands. He had even given her my corsage! Her hand was on his shoulder....

It was not as if he was my boyfriend, because he wasn't.

He was a date.

A date for me, for my Prom!

He had taken the tickets and called me babe!

I inhaled, but before I could move ...

It was like in the movies and in slow motion...

You know when things happen and you can't believe you are seeing what you are seeing but you can't look away? Not even if you tried?

A man, in an Army uniform stopped the two, turned Dwayne around and laid him out with one hit!

Tony McGregor. Pricilla's boyfriend!

The music stopped.

Everyone was watching.

"If you get up I will kill you for touching my fiance!" The voice carried even though it was low and deadly sounding. Dwayne did not get up. He stayed down.

Of course every one of us girls now gushed as we watched Tony, all 6' of man, go down on one knee, holding out a box. "I could not get a ticket or a tux after paying for this, I may be hauled out of here by the MP's since I am supposed to be on base, but honey will you...."

Pricilla was squealing and grabbing him, hugs and kisses and no one was watching Dwayne. The man's white tux now covered in blood, a good smack in the nose will do that. A nose will bleed forever.

I turned to Ms. Bremer. "Never mind! Don't need a thing, that show was enough for the price of the tickets!"

Two weeks later, Tony and Pricilla tied the knot in front of a Judge. She only dated Dwayne to make Tony jealous. She wanted him back anyway she could. Sure, it was at my expense, but at least I found out what kind of person Dwyane was.

Poor Tony had endured boot camp and then finally getting to come home before shipping out and found out that Pricilla had concocted this to get his attention? Well, he must love her.

Chapter 2

Mom passed away a year later in a car accident. She was off on her yearly *thing* with her sister. The two were close in friendship but not by miles as Pop would say. So yearly mom would head out to Sherie's place and they did their sister thing.

Pop and I had been out checking stock, mom was visiting. Aunt Sherie who lived in Billings there were lots of stores to shop and they got their hair done. All kinds of sister-things. I was a bit jealous, no siblings to share with but Pop and I would give her a send-off and knew that she enjoyed every minute.

I was more hair in a ponytail, blue jeans and boots type.

We were riding and checking fences in the north end and we had just passed the Stone-mas. It vibrated hard enough to spook the horses. I had been beside it lots of time but you had to put your hand on it to feel it vibrate.

Pop got down and inspected the huge rock, looked at me and said, "Something is wrong."

This rock had been here for ages. Great-grandfather said that one day it appeared. Just appeared at the edge of the field near the heavy pines.

I measured it and checked it out for a science project when in Junior High. Chipped a chunk off and found that it held magnetic properties but was made of nothing that I could find to compare it to. The chunk still sits on my dresser. I would hold it and it felt like it warmed up but never vibrated in my hand. You had to touch the full rock to *feel* it vibrate.

It made for great stories. The Scottish side of our family heavily believed in folklore and this rock became ours.

But it never vibrated like this before, well, not that I noticed. It is not like it is *that* close to the house for us to keep an eye on it. But the Brahmas would, at times, face that way and you could see them wiggle their ears as if they were listening....

When we got back we got the news about mom. A message on the machine to call mom's sister.

Cell phone reception when out checking the fences or the land is jumpy. At times you get surprised when your cell rings while riding.

What we got was bits and pieces until we got to talk to Uncle Phil. Sherie was too broken up. A car accident. Mom had been alone and on her way back home. She had just left Billings.

Pop took off that evening but we later found that she died on impact. Quick and painless.

Chapter 3

I sit here again on the porch, alone. February. And it is cold again. Well February in Montana you expect it to be cold. Nothing new there. The air is crisp, the sky full of twinkling stars and for some reason I feel good.

Feel safe.

I am on my cell phone planning with Freddie our annual get-to-gether. The SuperBowl is tomorrow. 02012015. My turn is next year.

Me and my friends take turns having it yearly.

Gonna be fun.

Freddie, still single also, runs a ranch by herself, Llamas. Weird looking little guys but their hair? She sells their hair for yarns and their poop for fertilizer. Did you know that Llamas will poop in the same place all the time?

No worry about 'accidentally' stepping in one. And, they are pebbles, like deer or rabbit poop. Who knew? And who knew how much that hair sold for! I can understand why she is doing that. And to see those cute faces as they stretch their neck and look at you. Honestly, adorable, just adorable.

Not like I plan on changing things here. Nope.

That is how I see my 'babies'. Adorable.

To have a newborn look at you with those huge eyes and floppy ears. A milk face and, well I give a sigh and fall insta-love with them. Each and every time.

But you have heard the phrase, *a face only a mother could love*. Ya, Brahma. Huge heads, big eyes and long eyelashes. Strange but to me, not. I look into their eyes and see their soul.

They don't hide behind anything. A mama will look at her young one and you can see the *words fly*. The youngster would then bounce off and away or hang their head and come over to her.

Any hoo.
We will be congregating at Freddie's place and watching that big screen, was that an 80" TV? Well, I did not measure it but we will all see it in all it's glory tomorrow afternoon. Sucker takes up a full wall. For some reason Freddie had to have it.

I remember the day it was delivered, a massive thing. And the guys hauling it in and hanging it up were not bad either! Freddie had her room totally revised. She had a wall removed, then a huge slider placed on the outer wall. The TV now is across from the sliders and that nice deck.

I wonder if that is so she can watch it from her deck? Hummm. Get some sun and still see a movie. Not-too-bad. The woman is inventive even if she drinks like a fish sometimes.

Not many who graduated with us stuck around this area, unless you worked on your parents ranch or worked in town or got your own little spread. My 'little' group still lives around here and we have planned this every year.

A time where we can act like ourselves and there is no one that will *tell mama*. Nope. We can laugh and joke and become young again. Like when we graduated and still drink. I have enough space for if anyone cannot drive home, they can stay here. Three guest rooms, the den where the couch flips into a bed and you can count on the recliner. The living room has a couch that everyone loves.....

But, that is next year. And I am prepared.

I have baked loads of goodies every night this past week and froze them. Mom had a 'thing' for baking and I learned some of it. Thank you for her huge box of recipes! I may not be as good as she was, but my stuff comes out OK.

Lots of 'small' breads. People love those things and baking several different kinds, it works for me. Banana bread. English loaf. Raisin bread. Also a fruit kind.

Also tiny pies. Mom said that it is an English thing. I can get away out of anything with those tiny pies.

Larger than a tart and full of fruit. And I, of course, had to look it up, and she is correct again. So, I have bunches of breads and pies for the party. Some Scotish treats are added so I have loads of stuff in the freezer. Just have to remember to thaw them out in time!

Finger foods are fun. Tiny desserts to enjoy. Never had anyone turn them down.

The gang will be hanging out again. The guys, well we all are older. Two are married now and one is seriously looking. Freddie rolls her eyes when he starts on 'who is new in town.'

If it is a male, *she* knows that sooner or later he will be at her little ranch. The guys kinda look out for us. You know, sending a guy to see an actual ranch that is ran by an actual female who lives alone and is of reasonable age and probably looking for a guy. (Yes, I heard that little confab Tyler said when he had no idea that Freddie and I were standing behind him.)

I snorted and nearly shot my beer through my nose!

So no, not concerned when they 'pop' over and haul a newcomer with them. Ya. It happens. Now, if we had tossed a female out and into their faces? Nope. And I was not about to start.

I actually don't leave the ranch that often. Well, when the circuit gets to Montana. I don't haul the Brahma's too far from home. And I handle them myself. I bring in someone to cover the ranch when I am gone. But there are times when one or both of my guys are *requested* and I get the full treatment. Room and board. N-i-c-e.

I look out and enjoy the afternoon quiet. My Brahmas are resting. I have two that will drop soon. Been watching them like a hawk. Daisy, this will be her very first and she is skittish.

The temps have been in the teen's during the day. And yes, I check the weather often. This is the mountains and we are a ways north here. The weather channel is my best friend. Radar checks at least twice a day.

And the animals. They sense this stuff, so I keep an eye on them also.

I check on the 'girls' then the generator in the back. Making sure that no matter what, they will be warm and snuggly. And no, don't ask, but I will let you know right now that there is not an air conditioner attached to the barn. I love the critters but hell, that is a wee bit much! The angle of the barn gives it an easy breeze when opened in the summer months. It works.

I enter the house from the wide wrap-around porch. The place had not changed much since mom died. We talked, Pop and I. Why change what works? There were the two of us, we had looked and talked of changes then vetoed it.

The small table sits between two benches where we have had breakfast since I could walk. Dad built the table to fit there. Sometimes when the bench can't hold the overflow of cooking, that big table is used. But now? Now we would sit and eat our meals there since it is just us.

Now, it is just me.

I can't remember the last time I sat at the big table.

I look around at the soft worn wood floors. Mom loved them. Taught me what to do to keep them in nice shape. If I wanted and was in my stocking feet, I could *skate* all over.

The windows have curtains that she had made. But the large windows in the front? She bought those and got those fancy rods. Black with large finials. She said they looked Scottish so she got them. A fancy black hooked thing. Nice. Pops liked them and that is all that counted.

If mom made it, he liked it. They were like that. She would hem and haw over garden ideas. Pop would add something and she would nearly clap her hands. I remember how much they loved each other.

You can see them in every room. Grandma took lots of photos. A picture here or there of them sitting on a blanket near a stream. One of mom on a horse with her hair flowing. I know Pop took that one. Him and her sitting at a 4th of July picnic holding hands. Memories all over the place.

Pictures of Pop when he was young. Lots of me with 4H-ribbons.

And of all the other people that ever lived here. Several are in black and white but the family of McWyntr is here. Odd that each generation only had one child.

The place is two-stories. Large. Built for a family. Someone had a grand idea. But the structure is solid and the only changes made were furniture or curtains. Couches and chairs come and go. Curtains fade and get replaced. But wood? It lasts and lasts.

There is a dining room with a huge table that opens more when you put the leaves in. This is for full meals or when company is over.

Mom wanted lots of kids, but only had me. I called it lucky, she laughed and shook her head. The home was built by great-grandpa and great-grandma. Four bedrooms upstairs plus the master. Downstairs was a huge back family room, the den or office, then an open living room, dining room and kitchen.

A working ranch. Ready for family or in our case guests.

There were always high-hopes for kids running around but each generation only had one child. I was the only female. So the McWyntr line ends with me. Unless I can find a gullible guy who will change HIS last name.

Na. Not going to happen.

That summer after Pop's death I rode out to the Stone-mas, got down and stood there. I was mad or just plain pissed at it. Yes, pissed at a damn rock. A rock that sat there and vibrated. No magical powers. No UFO. No tiny people who zipped around. I stood there and screamed at it.

"You do know that I am a female? The **last** of the line? Do you plan on doing anything about it?"

But I didn't get an answer.

Hell, I didn't know what would happen. It's not like I was gonna turn into a boy. Ya, that would have been hilarious.

OK. Not funny at all. But hell, I felt better for it. I have not been able to really grieve that my parents were gone. So screaming at that damn rock allowed me to feel better and to release the hatred I did not know I was holding. Mad at being alone. Mad that the ones I loved and thought would be here until very old and ……

That I was alone in this world.

Ok, I have some great friends. If I wanted I could call anyone of them and hang out. And I did. Just not that often lately.

There is a cool bar in town that we had hung out at even before we could drink. But the line-dancing was fun. Getting out and dancing. Hang out with friends. Some nights are just - plain - great. I figured I lived a normal life. I had my home, folks, friends, school and I went to rodeos just like everyone else around here.

When I rode away from the rock. The one we called Stone-Mas. I thought about that. And also wondered IF I would have been there when Pop passed away, did the rock vibrate the same it did for mom?
    I will never know…..
    I was at the hospital, sitting with him and holding his hand when he passed.
    If I had been at the ranch would I have seen the Bahamas look out towards the rock? They are sensitive actually.
    Freddie's dad had sent someone over to feed them for me when I stayed with Pop. And no one had said anything odd had happened.

Chapter 4

My phone chimes with a text from Tyler. He is now the sheriff of our small town. I look, something about a weather-front coming in. I reply thanks. I pull up the information on my laptop and read it.

Good to know. Freezing temps / Storm possible / Ice accumulation.

It is good having friends in high places. I am grateful for the information. I have babies that may drop soon so I need to dust my butt off and double check things before going to bed.

Tyler married Sherie and they have two kids. It is like old days when we get together, Tyler and Sherie need time off from the kids also. That is another reason why we have the party.

We all need a break from the winter. A break from routine and because, It Is The Super Bowl!

Sherie's mom will be there to babysit at their house. She will stay over and in the meantime spoil those cute little buggers silly. I love it when they take time to visit.

Family.

I smile as I pull up the weather app to check again. A rancher depends on these things. So far, I have kept the Brahma's sheltered. Had a scare of roof collapse one winter with the heavy snows but since then, all is good.

Just got my last two boys back. They had been trailered here from the train station in Billings. They spent a week in Vegas. I could not go with two pregnant ones here and so close to dropping. The vet is on stand-by if anything happens.

I missed trailering them and being there. My other guy, 'Come-N-GetMe' is older now and retired, other than playing with the ladies, he is staying put. The others are only 2 and 3 years old and love bucking their riders off.

Yes, this was late in the season. Actually the circuits were over, done. Then this.

My '*big guys*' had the honor of getting picked for the 15-15. The top 15 bull riders vs the top 15 bulls. Of course I watched it and cheered for my 'babies'.

Cotton Candy is named for his pinkish skin.

DevilMayCare is all black like his daddy, Come-N-GetMe.

Me, the proud mama. Cheered and was happy to see that the record is still good. No one has ridden them for the full 8 seconds. To watch or if you are the rider, it seems long. For me to be there, ring my hands and hope that all goes well.

Hell I know what happens out there. They get shoved, prodded and pushed around. I don't know what goes on in their heads when it happens but when I get to them, stand there for a moment so they see me and smell me.

Know that they are back to normal so I can walk them back and talk to them. Tell them how proud of them that I am and how happy that they are safe. Accidents happen. A broken leg from landing wrong could happen. I worry.

They were brought home here around noon last week, I was excited as the guys do travel well, but hardly ever without me. I coddle them. I know. And I am like the mom who let her boys go for a weekend trip.

This one lasted longer than a weekend. They got picked up and taken to the train station, from there to Vegas. Then stayed in Vegas during the illumination rounds. I was told that their handler was kind. But who really knows?

I was nervous waiting. The driver had called when he picked them up in Billings. I hear it and watch as the truck backed in. Coming to a stop a wrangler jumped out, a new guy I never met. He moved and pulled a cattle prod out from behind the seat. He saw me and "Careful ma'am. Got some mean ones here."

In my mind I saw him, pain hit me. Were they treated like this when away? Some idiot using a cattle prod?

The driver who she recognized, got out and shook his head, "Ms. Gemma. I tried to tell him that they change when they get back home. But the boy's head is like a brick wall."

I laughed then as I relaxed, then turned and gave a shrill whistle.

The wrangler stopped. Turned to me and watched as I moved to the back of the trailer. "Now, *you* step back and let me release those two. You don't get between a mama and her babies."

I nearly laughed when his jaw hit the ground.

"I need to protect…."

"If you hold real still and close your mouth. I will not let them charge you."

He did shut up but he watched. Still held that stupid cattle prod. God how I hated those things. They shot actual volts into the animal's hides. Painful. I had witnessed it several times at rodeos and at auctions. Makes me want to scream.

I pulled the pins from the door, swung it open and dropped down the ramp. I moved and saw Devil-May-Care turn on a dime, he snorted and stomped. He was still on pins and needles from his time away from home.

From the look in his eye he was ready to do some damage to someone.

The wrangler moved to me and I hissed at him, "you just touched their mama."

He turned white, "What?"

"I am their mama num-nuts. Now don't move again until I get them unloaded." I ignored him and walked up the ramp and sang, "You are my sunshine, my only sunshine….." Had my fingers crossed that they had not been too stressed and remembered me and my voice.

Anyone could see the change come over the two big guys. They shivered once, lowered their heads for me to ruffle their hair and rub between their eyes. I unhooked their leads. And I let go of a deep breath. My babies were back.

They nudged me and I said, "Did that bad man scare you?"

Cotton Candy snorted and now my hand was full of yuck. I did not mind. Just shook it off my fingers as I took a hold of the harness around their heads. I looked behind me at the wrangler, "Get back inside the truck, I got them." And 4 tons of animals followed me like puppies once I had them turned. Moving in line down the ramp. I hummed our song and they followed all the way into the barn.

I got them in, secure as they walked into their section then to their stall. I had placed fresh hay food and water earlier for them.

No one understands the connection I have with my animals. To me they *are* family. I treat them as such and talk to them. I don't have anything to share other than love. With no siblings, I shared my love with these animals. Mom may have tsk-tsked me but I still did it.

They grew up with me playing with them, washing them, taking care of them. Talking to them and laughing at their antics. Watching a huge animal like that roll in the grass or charge into the stream? Ya. Fun shit.

Me on horseback and them all running across the pasture. No one understands unless they were there.

No, I have not once brought them inside the house. No, I have not let them do anything they want. No and no. I respect them and they in turn respect me back. I trust them not to hurt me and they know I would not harm them. Mutual.

I know that they follow me. But look, these are all huge animals. If one stops and stands on your foot, it is gonna hurt and most likely break a bone or two. So why take chances? I know my boundaries and they know theirs.

Pop and I would trim their horns annually or when needed. Even those babies have growth spurts. Check hooves and legs when it is muddy so the animals are clean and dry. Keeping them healthy, they depend on us and now - they depend on me.

I never ride them. Nope. That is one thing that makes me different. They think of me as 'mama'.

And I never kick something that works.

The gentle ones, and we have had several. They are trained to pull wagons. You've seen them. Some have Long-horns pulling wagons and some have a Brahma. I have 'open checks' maybe once a year for buyers to come and inspect my stock. They like the younger ones, easier to train. And now with the ranch gaining a rep, they may be looking for their next rodeo wonder.

I don't know why, but if you have this huge creature with doe eyes look at you, you just want to hug them. Even if they weigh more than our truck. I look at my animals differently. They are not *stock* but animals that are my friends.

Annnd that may be what keeps the boys at bay. Sit and talk about brahma bulls half the night and it turns guys off. Unless it is one that knows me and those guys are already hooked-up.

Not like I was comparing the two. I love my ranch, nuff said.

The herd was larger when it was the two of us. I was sorry to see them go. Selling the young ones when they were ready. Easier on me. So now, there are 10 with two on the way.

Chapter 5

Scott has a ranch north of me. And he teaches at the school in town. He raises buffalo. People have signed up over a year in advance for his buffalo meat. Then there are the hides and horns. The guy may be rolling in money but he still acts the same. Well, not the same before entering the service. The man we got back was quiet and kept to himself.

Buffalo and him? Similarities.

A few fancy restaurants in Billings truck on over to pick a steer or two.

Profitable. He keeps the 'crowds' down due to the fact that these animals spook easily. They are big, hairy and smell to high heaven. Glad that I don't bathe those suckers. But Scott said laughing, *'their hygiene is up to them.'*

And every ranch has either a stream or pond on their land, it works both ways. The animals get to rinse off and owners get to use it also. At times a river has prime fishing. Another reason to get together.

There are other ranches around. Call themselves consortiums. Me and fellow ranchers look at them with disdain.

Big ones with fancy names and well, I don't really associate with them much. They bred and it is only a business for them. I heard things when in town but chose to keep away and keep to my own self. Besides, they are further down the road from me, so no problem-o.

I hang close to my ranch, see friends and go to church at least once a month. (Well I try). But the old school gang, we communicate often. Hit our favorite bar in town, catch up on the gossip and dance until our legs are weak, sweaty and pooped.

Know what each other is doing and keep an eye open for each other. I look again at the weather app. Looks like we will either get the full brunt or - possibly it will miss us. With these valleys, it is hard to say.

I love the mountains surrounding me. I see the snow capped peaks and watch as by mid-summer the snow is gone.

I still check the sky. Watch my herd. *They* also read the weather and I will act accordingly with both. Good ranching takes more science than anything. I don't raise crops, I purchase from my neighbors. We work together. Know what others are planting and will assist when needed.

I move. Standing, wipe off my ass and do what is needed.

Check their food supply. Both hay and grains.

I tickle the mama's necks and complement them on their babies. Last but not least, I double check all generators. Two for the barns now and one for the house. Primed and ready.

If something trips them, they will come on and all will be safe. My pregnant mama's can relax and know that I will keep them safe and warm. No lower than 50 degrees inside the barn, stable temps equal happy mama's. Yes I know that they have tough hides, but the young ones don't, not yet.

All I need to do is dim the lights when leaving.

Keep it basic and not let them even think I am worried.

They know me too well and can read me like a book.

The big guys watch me get ready to go out the door. OK, I may be worried....

Once inside the house I check the supplies. Flashlights. Candles. Unplug anything not needed. Basic precautions. And I have the rifle ready and loaded. A revolver next to the paper towel roll and I have one in an ankle holster.

Weird weather brings out weird shit.

while dealing after a tornado a few years back. A group of crazies attacked the town. Tore through in pickups and threw rocks into store windows. They did get caught and fined.

Probably still working it off somewhere....

And there are the wild animals. Even they do the weirdest shit when the weather is *uncommon*. But, hopefully they know better than to attack my barn. Wolf vs bull? That may be a laugh. Maybe I should install cameras inside…... Na.

Scott texted me and asked if I needed help. Buffalo are carefree, even in this weather. I smile, "Maybe tomorrow to get the food over to Freddies."

I get a "*Yum*," back with rolling eyeball emojis.

I giggle and shake my head. The man likes his food. And he still works out and stay's fit.

No one knows what happened when he was in the service. He knows that if and when he wants to talk, one of us will be there for him. And now he has someone he trusts. He met with Marcie when he came home on his last leave, love at first sight. They plan on getting married soon. We are all thrilled and happy for him. To have a partner, someone to share with, is a good thing.

Being a rancher is at times busy or you have nothing. But having someone for a partner is nice. And there, we have Marcie. She is shy. Came here to teach. They met and have been together since.

Scott is a teacher at school in town, loves history and has given me details about the Stone-Mas. Asked about the name when we were young, I told him that great-gramps said it showed up around Christmas and it is stone.

Mas-Stone was weird so it became Stone-Mas. But it has been kept secret. Not like it is a moon rock or a meteor. Although it could be something like that. But why call in the scientists and have them haul it away? It is good to us and now, it is something that just *belongs* here.

Scott looked at me funny when I told him.

Pop only shook his head at us.

But I took him to see it anyway. Good thing he could ride, we didn't have an ATV or anything. Just the horses or drive a truck back there. And I was only 12 at the time, so horses it was.

Scott did not mention food, so maybe he is getting the refreshments. Guys and beer. OK he may bring chips. Freddie has the list of who is bringing what. Ain't my job until next year.

The wind picked up after dinner. I looked outside often but the sky was as clear as a mid-summer night. The stars were bright, sharp and there was a sliver of a moon.

The wind howled, I heard it on the roof.

Metal is loud but safe due to fires. But stuff like this gets amplified. I did have a bladder inserted first to quiet the sound, but times like this? Makes you shake your head and do your best to ignore it.

I go upstairs, set my alarm. Brush my teeth, wash my face, take my hair down into a side braid, and go to bed.

5am is ranch time to get up.

Chapter 6

A noise.
The wind?
I look at the clock by the bed, 0202, then it goes dark and does not come back on.

Well shit.

Silence.

Not expecting that.

Weird. Well after all that wind earlier….

The curtain is open a smidge, outside the mercury lights flicker. My mind asks, 'why?'

I went to bed late, finishing up a few baked goods, and needed my rest to be included into the festivities and all that with the party. And, now I will have circles under my eyes from not getting enough sleep. And I know that I will not be the only one with eye circles.

This weather causes everyone restless nights and you don't need to be a rancher.

I move.

I have to check the stock.

My bread and butter…

The last tornado was in '95.

I remember the town after the tornado, the high school had the roof torn off.

We also had a blizzard that closed nearly all the roads for two days about four years ago. That sucker was no fun.

Here I was, alone and shoveling snow nearly 4' deep to get to the barns. A girls gotta do what a girls gotta do.

I am moving getting dressed as I leave the room.
Tossing off my tank top and boy shorts.
Put on my bra and panties.
Insulated underwear and thermal top, tube socks.
Another pair of socks. These go up and over the thermal bottoms and up pass my calves.
I grab my thick coveralls with wool inside from the hook on my closet door where I hung them last night. Stay prepared as Pop would say.
Turn and head for downstairs. In the dark
Pulling my hair up into a high pony.

I move through the kitchen to the mudroom. Here I can see out the window to the barns. I squint as I look. The outside lights flicker and go off.
Is that fog?
Swirling mists float by.
I tilt my head and keep moving.

The big mercury lights flicker off and on. I know the generators will be kicking in soon if the electricity is off for a full minute. It's the on and off that drives me bonkers. Ya want to count to 60 and then start all over again. Would do that when younger. Stand on the wide porch protected by the over-hang. The storm had gone through and I would watch and count for the generator to kick on.

But not now. Right now I want to get to the barn. I remember the ice I walked over last night when I did my last check. Knowing that the steps are wood, could be nasty.

I pull my boots on, pull a sweatshirt on and down over the coveralls, then my baseball cap, flip hair through the hole. I feel like a little kid that mom dressed.

Yarn cap is next to pull down over the baseball cap and cover my ears, then pull the hoodie up over everything. Pulling the ties as I get it adjusted over my head and knot it under my chin as I continue looking outside.

My arm instinctually reaches for the large scarf.

Wrap the muffler around my neck so I can pull it up over my face and pull my Carhart jacket on. Pull that hood up. Wind-chill on skin, burns and sucks all the moisture out.

Last I am jerking leather gloves over the jersey ones, I open the door and step out. Ready.

I look up out the window of the door for the stars. See nothing. Nothing but fog. Thick. Swirling mists.

Fog?

Remembering the scary movies. The crap that happens. *'Don't leave the house. Don't go out there....'* I feel like someone is using a smog machine that I saw at the theater when it was the production of some play.

I look at the barn, there is a huge thermometer hanging on the side and…

What? That can't be right. 41 degrees?

It was negative 5 when I checked before going to bed around 10.

Stepping off the porch, I move to the barn. Listening to the animals. They will make noise if shit is happening but I hear nothing. They are not concerned or because their temp inside is set to stay constant. Or….

I can't go there. I know that they are ok. Safe.

I move and just walk. The ice that was there earlier is gone now. Not even any water over ice to cause trouble. I look up and around and still can't see much. But the barn is closer and I get to it.

I think of all the old movies, where someone is walking through fields of mist to get to their castle. OK. Pop and Granddad's stories are getting to me…..

The mist swirls around me. Thicker now and I can just make out the barn. The door easily opens, it is never locked. Hell if someone did sneak in, one look at who lives there and they would be gone! I know for a fact that the bulls would not allow a stranger to enter and with two very pregnant females? No freaking way.

And since their stalls doors are not locked…. One nudge and they are out.

By the time I enter I am sweating. It was not that far, but I am overdressed right now. Whew! Peeling things off when I enter, I move around and check everyone as I strip off the large coat and scarf, sweatshirt….

Toss the carhart, scarf and things over a rack holding the pitchforks and rakes. My head swivels to see if all is right with everyone in here. My breath which had been faster coming over, now slows as I take in the looks from sleepy animals.

OK. I woke them up. Sorry.

The mama's are first, and I see they are with their babies in the larger pens. Not too bothered. They look at me as if I am doing something stupid. And I probably am. But this is what I do. These animals depend on me.

Young one's sprawled out and slept. Tails flicker than an ear but they stay asleep. Their mom's look at me and I feel stupid for even coming out. I shrug at them and keep walking. Checking everything.

They are in the semi-light and doing just fine. Trying to sleep and….

Well, I am here…

A bull or two bellow soft to ask me why I am disturbing them.

My phone buzzes first, then rings. I jerk it out.

Tyler. Our sheriff.

"What do you see up there? Called Scott, he has ice and low temps."

"Fog, thick fog and 41 degrees. Wind has stopped."

"Crap" He inhales. "It is freezing here. Wind still creepy sounding and ice on the branches. We may lose power." Then he stutters, "You have 41?"

"I am ready to peel off more clothes here. Way overdressed. The animals aren't bothered at all."

Just then there was a loud clap of thunder.

Gemma looked out the windows and noticed that the whole sky lit up.

"I saw that from here," Tyler said in a loud whisper. Why he whispered is odd but hell, the whole place lit up like it was noon on a bright summer day.

"Listen, I will call back," Gemma then hung up, made sure the phone was inside an inner pocket and moved closer to the windows. She was **not** going to talk on the phone if there was lightning going on.

Wives tale or not.

Looking out she saw fog and…..

Was that a man?

She blinked, looked and saw a figure moving - and then several others…....

Chapter 7

The fighting was hard and heavy. He had some injuries he was sure. Blood ran down him but not all of it was his. His sword arm was tiring, he moved a step back and turned, looking for his brothers in arms.

Doing his best not to trip over an injured man or a dead one. There was no time to check one if injured. The area was full of moans and groans. A grunt here then quiet. His heart went out for those injured due to the fact that aid was not coming soon.

There was hope of seeing them still standing. The sorrow hit him when he saw so many down. An arm reaching out - for help? Some now stiffening from death. The smell of blood was strong. A battlefield. A place of death. Scottish bodies as well as English.

He squinted, searched in the light rain swept area and his heart gladdened when he spotted them. They still lived! His heart pounded now, not fearing death of his brothers as with those so near. Finding them, seeing them still standing, his heart beat faster and gave him strength.

It would be dark soon. They were far away from any tree line, no support to aid them and nowhere to rest. This worried him. No rest easily meant death. This was yet another day, and he was nearly dropping from exhaustion.

But they had to pull back. Needed to stop and regain their strength. And it had better be soon or all may perish.

The English fell back then came forward yet again and again.

Men not covered in mud and blood. Men fresh.

Coming from where?

In the midst of the drizzling rain he could see men coming close again. Yet another rush. Why weren't they backing down? Why weren't they tiring? Fresh troops from where?

Fearghas stood in a low area. Not quite a valley. Beyond him was the forest, if he could get back up yon hill he could find rest. Backing up was not a bad thing. It did not mean he was leaving the fight. But he needed rest and he needed it now.

As he looked around again he did his best to step back but not step on a body. Not knowing if the man was dead or alive. Seeing swords covered in blood. Spikes sticking out of bodies. A gruesome picture of once what was a pristine valley. Now one of pain and sadness.

He had seen faces And yet the English still came and fought. Why? Why was this village, this land so important that they sent so many to fight the Scots?

He moved back, withdrawing his knife from the now dead Englishman's chest as the man fell to his knees then fell forward. Knowing that his own body grew tired, and his heart no longer in the fight. So many lives lost on this field.

Sorrow and mournful cries would be heard from the village behind him when the many wives and mothers would come to claim the fallen bodies in the morning light. He knew that many waited in the treeline above him. Watching and waiting for a loved one to appear.

The valley that was once a gentle slope, green. One where children from the small town played.

He remembered rolling down a hill such as this when young.

But today, no two full days of fighting so far. Today's in the rain. So close after the holiday's. The priests were aghast at this. But Fearghas's mind was not on the priests with not.

The valley, now full of blood and death.

The clanging of swords. The grunts of the fighters and the sound of - death.

English were moving over bodies to get to the other side and fight more.

Scot's getting pushed back again and again, and doing your best not to fall over. His men, brothers.

They also saw him and did their best to move closer, stay in contact. Fearghas had to keep moving his blades, stay alive as the fog that now appeared got thicker and thicker. Men who kept fighting were coming from all sides.

He hoped upon hope that he could keep his wits and stay on his feet. Get a chance to back up and get a breath. Just one deep full breath. Aye.

Keeping his eyes sharp he watched. Calculated. Waited.

This was his fight. His old village was one that was attacked by these barbarians from another coast. His ma and da, now long gone, but here was where he had been born. He had been the youngest. The only lad. His sisters now with husbands and far away. I hoped they were safe from this.

Why? Why now?

He had heard that the English had quieted in their rush to subdue the Scots.

Odd that they attacked now. It was in the winter of a new year.

A flash of light. He waited for the thunder but nothing followed. A sound though, low and keening…. The sounds of those waiting for their loved ones, that was all he heard.

Pea soup fog, the thickest he had ever seen that now grew closer and closer.

He could not believe what he was seeing.

This was only getting worse and worse.

The drizzle or the mist. It was over him and he felt the chill now. His clothing was drenched. Parts not drenched with water were covered in blood and gore. His arms, his chest. Head hurting from it all along with the injury. The one where he nearly lost his head as the English swung and tripped over a body, thus turning his wrist so the flat side hit Fearghas.

It had taken him to his knees, that hit. But Fearghas had brought up his short sword and gutted the man. Shook his head, stood and fought some more.

This was day two or was it three of fighting? He had to rest soon. He stumbled, nearly fell.

His head rang from the injury, blood had run down the side of his face where now, it had slowed or stopped. His eyes moved, searching for his brothers again.

His arms were getting weak.

His chest gave him pain when he inhaled. A rib. Most likely broken.

Gashes on an arm. Cuts on his legs. He was battered but not yet broken. This land. The land of his Clan. It meant something to him. Not love but of brotherhood. Of Clans helping Clans. Friends and fellowship.

In a distance he could smell smoke. Fires started. Homes will be destroyed today along with families. The sadness hit him in the chest. He stood, legs shaking, knew that weakness meant death.

Was today the day he would face death? The land where he was raised?

The thought shook him to his core.

No. He was **not** ready to die.

His stance straightened. He again raised his swords. He looked and he saw his brothers get closer, he then heard some odd noise.

Cattle?

He must be tired.

This field of men fighting and dying, held no cattle. The village had a cow or two.

They were in a valley. A village nearby, a stream where earlier, much earlier he had drank. Washed blood from his face, from his arms.

It was but a small break.

He had seen his brothers and had spoke. That was some time ago.

Nothing was here but men fighting……

How long would this keep up?

Another flash, this one much brighter, he had to squint it was so bright and … a building appeared?

His nose told him he saw was no longer in the field. This field.

His body still moved the broadsword in one hand, his shorter sword in the other, he had to stay alive….

He smelled animals now more than blood.

The temperature was dropping.

Something was Fearghas's head whipped around, finding his brothers and giving a signal to come. Group-up.

Was he the only one who hears this change?

Where before there were sounds of swords clashing, of men grunting as they fought, the smell of blood that blended with the rain and mud.

He saw four fighters advancing on him, yelling as they charged forward… then, they were gone.

Silence surrounds him. His hair on his arms tingling from the passage from there to - he had no idea of where he was.

His brothers, they stood together, making a circle, slowly turning to fight or….

Something appeared in his vision, the fog split, an opening!

Fearghas was moving, they all moved and heaved their big bodies through. He had heard of these 'portals' but this was his first. He had no idea of what was on the other side, but it had to be better than this field so full of death.

Anything to save him and his brothers……

Anything.

To stay in this field full of death, knowing that they may not survive. This had to be done. Wishing for a chance at life, he moved. A choice was made.

Fearghas now stopped and stood.

The air here was chilled.

His chest heaved as he caught his breath. There was still pain in breathing but not as much. His body tensed. Waiting. The English bastards were out there, charging....

His eyes moved, watching. Then his head turned as he tried to understand what the hell he was seeing......

Fearghas moved his swords slowly, cleaving through the air, fog moved, lifted swirled and the sound he heard was ... silence. His men stood near, each looking, scanning, sniffing. They now made a slow circle, their backs in the center, facing out and watched.

But for what? The chill made the hair on his body stand up.

Another clap of thunder sounded, this time the ground shook.

Fearghas knew the portal, if that was what it was, now was closed. It had opened and now - closed. Was this all a trick?

Where was he now? He closed his eyes and asked the God's, *'was this a good choice?'*

The English, were they coming? The valley? He turned, nothing looked familiar. No green, no valley and no bodies near his feet. No grunts from fighters. No swords hitting, clanging, ringing in his ears was from his head injury not from sounds surrounding him.

The blood that had been running down his face from the injury he received, now had stopped. He looked at his left arm, the one holding his dagger and saw the slash, it was now healing.

The slice had been real but this? The pain from receiving it, real. That also was receding.

Looking at his brothers, really looking at them he saw that their injuries were also healed or healing. How odd was that? But it was good. Aye. No one was bleeding to death here. Again, where was here?

Had the portal healed them as they came through? Is that how it is done? He had heard stories when young. His da said they were *light and untrue.* When he asked why, his da said that it is unproven.

Was this because those that went through ne'r returned?

Fearghas wanted to talk, ask the men to check themselves, but seeing what he saw now? All thoughts of talk disappeared.

The English could be hiding in the fog. This could be all some kind of trickery.

All knew that the English harbored witches to do their dirty work.

What place was this?

And where were they?

The green was gone. Here it was white.

Chapter 8

Fearghas, his name meant *Supreme choice*. He stood 6'4" tall. Age 5 and 20. Thick, long black hair and brown eyes. He was strong-built. Two bands surrounded his arms at his biceps to show his order in standing, showed he was of higher rank, and one wide band over his chest for holding his sword, chest now bare other than the sheath for his sword, he wore his kilt and boots that were tied high up on his calves.

His broad sword in one hand and a short sword in the other. His dagger on his hip. He was standing, watching his surroundings. Aware of the change and not liking it. His body was tired, weak from fighting and…

This. This he did not understand.

Barra, his name was *'fair head'*. Age 4 and 20. He stood at Fearghas's left at 6' tall with blonde hair and blue eyes. Also with a band around his bicep, bare chested, kilt, boots. Broad sword and dagger. Concerned because the muddy field was no longer under his feet.

Not understanding the smells that hit him. Not fond of cattle after being knocked silly by a steer when age 10. His legs tired from the long fight. He wanted ale, needing his parched throat handled. He would wait until given an order to stand-down.

Branhubh, his name meant *black raven*. He was 6'6" black hair and nearly black eyes. Also dressed as Fearghas and Barra. Age 30.

He was shoulder to shoulder to Barra, also wondering what and where they just landed. His eyes flickered left and right. Not understanding what he was seeing. The wait for a body to race toward him with a sword or pike was nerve wracking.

Kon-chur, his name was *high will order*. He was Fearghas 1st in command. He was on the right of his leader. His teeth started to shatter from the chill, his chest was still in pain from the cuts he earlier received. Knowing one was on his back shoulder from a knife earlier.

When he looked down his body, he saw the blood had stopped. As the oldest at 1 and 30 and 6'6", he was also dressed similarly but with a wide band around his head holding his long hair off his face.

He stood with his shoulder near Fearghas, eyes clearing but trying his best to stay standing although his chest still pained him from that last blow he took. Looking down at his chest he feared a large gash but what he saw was - nothing. The knife had not penetrated?

Drostan, his name meant *French*. His ma loved books. At age 8 and 20, at 6', teased for not having hair on his face yet. He had brown hair that fell in ringlets down his neck and blue eyes.

Women would sit on his lap at the taverns and play with his curls as he drank.

Looking with wonder at the white now surrounding him and his brothers. His one true brother, Barra, he quickly glanced and saw that even covered in blood, no one seemed injured. Sweat was drying quickly in the cold air.

They all stood, breathed deep. Smelled freshness and no blood. No one came at them through the mist. They expected something, anything as they waited. The English they had fought just moments ago were now - gone?

Their breaths made mist in the air as they inhaled and exhaled from their mad dash through the portal.

They looked at each other as they moved as one. Stayed alert to their new surroundings. The oddity of it all.

Disheveled, bloody.

Swords still dripping blood, but….. Alive. Yes. Very much alive.

These men who had become brothers. They had lived and fought together. No real home, no family other than each other. Today they had been fighting the English who were again invading their land.

The battle had been brutal and they all did their best to stay alive. To back the bastards up, wanting them to high-tail it back home. Wondering how they would feel if this was happening in their yard?

These men, brothers, stood, moving in a slow circle.

Breathing heavy as they moved, keeping each other covered.

Feeling the stress of the last few days, knowing that the man beside them was as tired as they were. That their legs barely held them up.

Waiting for the fight to come to them. They had been fighting for their lives just moments ago. Found each other and followed as one moved.....

The chilled wind calmed, the lightning disappeared and the sounds of battle were - gone. Where had all the fighters gone? Not another Scot was near. Nor English.

Where was the battle if not here?

They were standing in … snow?

When had it snowed?

Where was the mud, the bodies the….

And where in the hell were those English bastards hiding?

They jumped when the area they stood in suddenly lit up.

The lights in the barnyard had come back on. Then the light beside the house came on.

Showing a structure that was unfamiliar to them. When had they been beside this structure? Was it a lodge that they had moved to? Its form was strange.

Looking up at the lights the men thought moons?

Three moons? And this close?

No.

The men growled at the unknown and were again at attention, ready to attack.

Chapter 9

In the barn, still looking out the window Gemma said, "Holy Moly! Did those guys just 'pop' out of nowhere or what?" She looked at the really huge men and saw their posture. Standing inside seeing them outside and wondering if she would wake up back in bed.

Sure as heck that she was dreaming all this because, well nothing was making any sense. Moving a hand she pinched her arm. OK. That hurt. And proved that she was not in bed sleeping through all this.

Yes, she was home.

Yes this was the barn.

Yes the animals were fine.

Yes the weather was screwed up. Tyler said it is ice and freezing in town which from here, is only 20 miles straight south. He said that Scott reported the same. But Gemma had 41 degrees and fog and now men?

So what the hell was going on here outside at her ranch???

Remembering a movie where she had watched reactions like this. This was Montana not the middle of a renaissance fair. Besides this was February. No renaissance fairs were around in the winter. Nope.

And there had been no talk about a movie being shot around here. Tyler would have said something....

This was not a movie, this was **her** ranch.

There was no director to yell 'Cut!'

No lights or cameras.

But they looked like Conon the Barbarian or the men who fought against the British ages ago ….

Yup, kilts and bodies, she remembered seeing Outlander and of course, who could forget Braveheart? Nope. These men, and yes she knew and understood that they were indeedy all man type men.

Oh hell yes..…

Only these men standing in her yard stood with paint on their faces and on their chests and… Warpaint.

These men looked muddy and … was that blood?

Gemma watched in a daze as they moved in a slow moving circle. Always looking out. Watching for? What? An animal to charge?

They moved huge swords in one hand and shorter ones in the other. And they were nearly naked standing there. THAT Gemma saw and understood. A kilt. Not much else.

And leather boot things strapped to their legs.

Gemma was sure those were kilts. Although she had never seen one personally. And this was up-close <u>and</u> personal.

OK, she was still hiding in the barn but give her points for that at least! Thank goodness she had not been standing outside when they appeared.

And - yes. They appeared. Poof. OK, no sound but hell they are here and so totally NOT from around here. No Siree. Pop would have a field day with..…

Gemma backed up and that was when she found out she was not standing there all alone. Cotton Candy was there and also looking out the window over her shoulder.

But where in the hell had *they* come from?

And why were they **here**?

At the ranch? Montana? Was this a joke of some kind?

Like, let's prank Gemma. She lives alone and hell, send a guy or two..…

Yes she had heard the thunder and seen the flash of lightning.

Yes she had heard of the folklore of men traveling through time.

Yes she had watched movies and read books. Time travelers. HBO and others had that. Not like she binge watched lately.

OK, she binge watched some shows….
But here?
Now?

Seeing the men looked up at the lights when they came back on and made noises as the lights do, and now … they looked at the barn.

Directly to where she was standing looking out. Her window.

Gemma gulped. Had *they* heard her? Has she spoken out loud?

OK.

Stories Pop told her.

There had been stories of 'old' he called them.

Of the rock formation on the ranch. That the rock was like those found in Scotland, old rocks. Rocks that appeared. Similar to Stonehenge but these rocks were from a great distance and individual. The talk of *rocks that roamed*.

He talked of fighters that also roamed and saved villages from Vikings or the English. Saving women and children from becoming slaves to the English. Spoke of the Clans and though mom would make a noise here and there, Pop swore that the stories were true and were meant to be shared.

Gemma had sat on the floor and listened to him when she was young.

Men who were warriors.

Warriors that wore kilts, the color of their Clans.

McWyntr was a clan. There were relatives of hers over in Scotland. He talked of his visits when he was very young. But later the ranch took more and more time. Visits no longer happened.

She had sat there and listened as she bit into an apple. The stories flowed and she listened. Pop said *one day, they would go see the old country*.

He would talk of the 'rock' on their property. But he actually told <u>her</u>. Said that the rock was special and had powers. That one day she would understand.

Pop would pass the history for her to share with her children.

Talked of special rocks showing up and allowing 'families' to pass. To move through time.

That this rock had not been <u>on </u>the property when purchased but <u>appeared </u>one day, or so Great-great-granddad had said. Said that the rock came through time and not from outer space. And said it came from Scotland.

Gemma believed that more and more when her friend Scott who wanted a chunk to send away to be analyzed.
    Said his father's father told them. And both of them believed.
    Stories of men who fought for safety, men who were ancient......
    The rock chunk never came back. Scott believed it was lost since no professor had written back. Was told that not many *listened* to a child. OK. They were 12, but if the rock was something important, would not someone call?

Gemma now watched the large men as they moved in a slow circle, keeping their backs protected.
    She swore she saw them sniff the air.
    Who does that?
    Did they smell the Bahamas? She was used to the smell but still she was sure that the smell was not *that* noticeable.
    Could they smell her?
    What was her next move?
    They were between her and the house.
    Well shit.
    Could she hide here? There was a place to sit. Even a cot.
    But not to eat. And....
    Well, that was answered when her phone rang. Loud and clear in the silence, even with it in her pocket.
    Shit. Shit.
    Gemma jumped and she saw them react.
    She saw them stop and look at the window she was looking out of. Their attention was fierce and their faces and bodies reacted, now, they were again warriors. Stone men now faced her and the barn. Boldmen. Fighters.

Fearghas barked out words. A language Gemma knew nothing of. But she knew one thing, <u>they</u> knew she was there or that someone was there, and now they looked at the barn, at the door, and they were fanning out.

Focused.

Well double shit.

Would they attack *her* if or when she stepped out of the barn? She was so bundled up they could not tell if she was male or female. She couldn't stay inside. And even though there was a side door. A run for the house, her vs them?

Ah that was a solid no.

She had nothing other than several shovels or a pitchfork in here for protection. The rifle was propped near the back door in the mudroom inside the house which was several yards away from her.

She did mute her phone as fast as she could. Worry about it later. Not even bothering to look who called.

Gemma closed her eyes.

Then something nudged her. She squeaked. Yes, squeaked. And nearly wet her pants! Gads!

Cotton Candy. He was <u>her</u> oldest Brahma. <u>Her</u> first baby. Come-N-GetMe was Pops more than hers and he was also the first boy they had and, he sired, Cotton Candy.

None wore their bells when here at home, so he snuck up on her. Well her attention was on the outside....

On the strangers in the yard.

Between her and the house.

No, not like she was distracted or anything.

As if a big 2 ton animal could sneak or even wanted to. They have hooves but aren't shod like a horse would be, so when he walked, it was quiet on the flooring covered with straw in most areas. His barn where he knew every square inch and moved where he wanted, when he wanted and now, he stood beside her. All warm and all as she looked out the window and worried.

Gemma looked over at him and curled her hand under his neck where it bulged below. He snuffed, moved his large head and looked out the window as she had done. These animals were so much a part of her and their actions even surprised her....

He snuffed again. She relaxed, knowing he would protect her. He had sensed that she needed him so he came.

And soon, if he called for it, the other big guys would be right there. Then there would be three. Gemma relaxed a tiny bit. Visualized her and three bulls walking to the house. Shielding her.

She shook her shoulders releasing the tension. That would work. But she would not do it. These guys were armed to the teeth and the bulls, even though they are tough. Gemma would not put them in danger.

The way Gemma had the barns set, the animals could move inside and outside with ease if needed. They learned as babies and mainly stayed where they were supposed to be. Their gates were set so if needed, a good shove and they would open. The younger ones played 'follow the leader' and at times frustrated Gemma to get them back inside at night in the summer.

But now? No.

They each had a pen and usually stayed there.

The females were in another section so there was no hanky-panky with them. Even though they would *nudge* that gate. And that one was steel, so the females were quite safe from the big boys.

Gemma knew she could be brave if the big guy was beside her. One bull and her would not be intimidating, right?

His shoulder was by her head even though she stood at 5'7". He was big and wide and battle scarred from cowboy spurs. And Gemma knew he could hold his own. Would she?

Could she ride him to her house and then jump off and be safe?

And that would be a no. Even knowing the bull, she had seen him in the ring and getting on him? Nope. Ain't gonna happen. Now was not the time to test their friendship.

She looked at the men standing outside her barn, "Cotton, what if I can't communicate with them? They don't look like anyone around here. And when one spoke, I did not understand him."

She looked at the tallest one with dark hair, a leather band around his head holding the long black hair back as he grunted something to one man beside him. This one had dark hair also but had a band around both biceps and his wrist. A cuff. A leather cuff. A fashion statement?

No.

These guys were not from around here!

This man now stepped forward. Was that blood on the side of his head?

He was also the one that she thought was the most....

Ya. He made her swallow and lick her lips when she 'checked him out' earlier.

He was the one that had her attention.

"Stop it Gemma. OK, him Tarzan, me Jane."

Her mom would slap her for the thoughts running through her head now. Gemma took a deep breath. Looked at the men. Looked at the door to her side, looked at Cotton Candy and said, "Let's get this over with."

She moved now, she had dressed again when she was ready to step out before the lighting and the guys and..... OK, she could do this with Cotton beside her.

She would simply step out, talk to them.

Gauge Cotton's reaction to them then get her ass inside the house and barricade the doors. There was a rifle in there and she knew how to use it. And a 911 call would not hurt.

Huh. Why hadn't she called Tyler earlier?

Ya. Get the strange men off the ranch, send them home. Everyone had a home and since she did not recognize even one of them....

Call out and find who is shooting a movie nearby and....

Then she would go to pee. She really needed to pee.

Cotton Candy would guard her.....

Gemma pulled on her clothing. Hands in her pocket, cell phone? Check. Ready as she will ever be, her mind made up. She was going out there, no longer hiding.

Chapter 10

The sound of the door opening on the lodge had their attention. Finally, movement. To find if what was inside was friend or foe. It was a farm of some kind. A farm that was unfamiliar looking.

Again, Fearghas looked around, he had stepped forward since they heard movement from inside after the odd noise. Odd looking wagons were nearby, he had looked and saw that they were made of metal and odd looking wheels, but that was of no concern at this moment.

There was the smell of animals and hay.

He knew of lodges that included animals. Winter. Aye. Animals and people lived together and the lodge would hold the heat. Safety for all.

His nose twitched when a softer scent hit him.

Was this the long house and females were inside?

Then the scent wafted, closer when the door opened and a figure stepped out, his legs wobbled and Kon-chur turned to him in question. Then went back on guard with the others.

Gemma moved with her bull Cotton Candy beside her. The huge Brahma did not stiffen at the sight of the strangers. He moved slowly, sniffed them himself but did not seem bothered. Like this stuff happens daily.

Gemma kept her hand on his lower neck, not needing anything else but contact with him to feel his reactions. He moved when she moved, stopped when she stopped. Her hand trembled and she saw a big eye look at her and back to the men.

Knowing that his skin would twitch when he 'felt' she would need to be warned. The skin on his lower neck held nerve endings and Gemma was using everything to her advantage. But he, being sensitive here, felt her tremor and that is why he looked at her. Gemma was now waiting.

If he lowered his head to charge Gemma was more than ready to make a run for the house and its safety. Yup. That was the plan. But here was the animal sniffing - Strangers. And dang if they were not sniffing her. Or were they sniffing him.

Her animals, they would be trusted. He would know if harm was there.

These strangers? No.

If necessary she would get back inside the barn. If they charged, Cotton would stop them, right? But as she stopped, he did not paw the ground or thunk a foot down harder than normal.

Gemma swallowed, watched the men, her eyes darting from one man to the other but going back to the one that stood just one step forward alone. Was he the leader?

Again she was covered from head to toe. Hiding her body in the clothing. They would harm a woman, maybe. Maybe because they could not tell she was a woman.

She felt her teeth chattering from the cold, her stomach clenched, but she moved forward with Cotton. Moving closer to her house.

Another step here, another step there.

The temperature was dropping fast.

She felt the cold so the nearly naked men should be feeling it also.

She glanced under the bulls neck at the side of the barn and saw the temp gage. Then back to the men standing around barely dressed.

She moved her one free hand as if to wave, stopped just as sudden when their swords moved. She kept the smile on her face but now watched the weapons in their hands.

"HI. Welcome to my ranch."

Well shit. That didn't work. Their eyes were still hard. Faces of stone looked back at her. They still looked pissed.

Was that a growl? How tense could a guy get? Lots, if these guys were any indication of it. They were stiff as statues, eyes darting around and acting as if they would charge. Shoulder to shoulder.

Arms moving with these large steel swords that flashed as the light caught them.

"You are safe here. I don't know if you understand me, but I will not harm you." her brain actually laughed at that line. How in the hell could she *harm* even one of them?

Fearghas watched the female. At least he thought it was a female. The clothing was confusing. She was bundled up because of the weather. But wore pants? Odd. Then there was her speech was odd.

But she was female. That he now knew. He could smell or sense her.

And why was his body reacting to t<u>his</u> female?

The smell had *caught* him and now that she was near, he wanted her closer. To place her inside their circle and protect her. Why?

The beast beside her looked relaxed. He saw the huge head move and the eyes lock on him. A head and body he had not recognized. But knew it was a bull and a male.

The animal type was unknown to him but Fearghas did not make a sound. And those sharp black eyes did not look mellow. Would she give the word for it to charge?

The beast looked docile but Fearghas did not trust it. It was with the female, protection? What female uses animals for protection?

What or who were they dealing with?

And where were they? The temp was dropping significantly and not one of them was dressed for it.

Not one thing looked familiar.

Where before there had been green grass and a hill…

It hit him then. This. This place was not Scotland.

He looked over at Kon-chur who nodded. The men relaxed as they now knew that only one person was here, who would leave a female alone?

Would her tribe or clan come home soon?

Would they try to fight?

The female did not hold a weapon.

The men had not smelled another human nearby, only this one. But several animals behind her in the low lodge.

Chapter 11

Well, things were <u>not</u> moving along the way Gemma thought it would. Since the men arrived, the temp was again dropping quickly. The fog was gone. The power was back on, she knew that because the sound of the generators stopped. It was still dark and she was still alone with 5 shirtless strangers holding weapons.

Strangers that looked at her like she was the one in the wrong place.

Seeing these shirtless men she felt bad for them. She watched them look around and up at the large Mercury lights. Seeing the swords she quit feeling so bad for them. Thinking *just quite fucking around and being threatening. Let's talk this out and I will call Tyler and he can pick you up and return you to where you belong. Which is NOT here.*

She watched them turn to her again and the one closest to her, now frowning. He looked up then back to her.

"Lights." Gemma answered, then she nearly slapped herself. Was this real? OK, they had talked in a strange language earlier. She would give them that much.

She touched her chest, moving her hand slowly as those huge swords again moved. She stopped, Well, she was the only person here. "Gemma." She touched her chest again, "Gemma".

She patted the huge bull, "Cotton Candy".

The one man who stood apart moved again, a step closer?

Gemma felt Cotton Candy twitch.

WTH?

But the bull did not stiffen, just the twitch. Did not lower his head. He only stared at one of the men. Were they communicating?

His eyes locked on the man but Gemma did not feel threatened as she had before.

Was <u>any</u> of this real?

Lightning flashed again, this time lighting up everyone and the area as if it was noon. Gemma felt the wave of thunder that followed hit her and she stumbled. Grabbing at Cotton Candy to stay on her feet.

Earthquake?

The men then talked to each other and …

She understood them. It came out a whisper, "I understand you." Her breath was frosty in the air.

Everyone looked at each other then her. And she knew then, they understood her also. OK. This is looking up now. Communication. Let them know to not attack. Yes. A good thing.

The man nearest her said, "Time."

Gemma looked at her wrist, checking her watch, "3am. Morning" (Had it been an hour already?)

He looked up.

"It's the lights, so I can see in the dark when I come outside to take care of my stock."

He nodded his chin in the direction over her shoulder. (So much for communication techniques.)

"Barn. They live there." He nodded again with a grunt, this time to her home.

"My home. I live there."

He frowned, looked around and sniffed.

OK. Barbarian, sniffing her ranch or sniffing her cattle or, maybe, sniffing her. No one does that now. Well they may but they get called on it!

Gemma giggled instead of out-and-out laughing at the group in front of her. These guys need serious help here. Then they turned to her and she stopped. Oh hell. They were holding those swords high and waving them around. What the hell.

The one again grunted. The others lowered the swords. He looked at Gemma and tilted his head. Another grunt.

Gemma wanted to put her hands on her hips but stayed with Cotton and spoke;

"I live alone. My parents, they passed away." And then she snapped her mouth closed. Why oh why did she tell them she was a-l-o-n-e???

She saw something in his eyes flicker. "Do you have family?" she asked.

"Non." He looked over his shoulder, "My men, my family."

Oh that voice. Rich. Deep. Were her toes curling in her boots? Even with several pairs of socks? Oh my. But I need to take baby steps here or …

'*OK. Seriously Gemma (straight talk needed here), you have been alone for too long. You have not been on a date in years. And hitting the bar in town with your friends does not count. Cowboys come and cowboys go. Ranches hire another and the world keeps turning.*

These guys and his buddies show up. On foot. And with no movie people around hoisting rigs with mics or all that shit. So what the hell? Gemma wants to turn around and spot the riggers that are hiding. This has to be a movie, right?

The guy talks and you get all gooey inside?

*Well hold that thought and hold your panties because something is not right in Denmark. These guys did not **just appear**.*

Gemma had seen his big muscled body shrug and also saw the other men relaxing their stance. The bull beside her snorted, turned and headed back to the barn, she swore she heard Cotton say 'warm … bed'.

Huh. Did that lightning have her understanding him also? And he was leaving her? She <u>knew</u> Cotton would be safe, there was a short hall, like a doggie door. He knew the way. But now, she was stranded here. Between the house and the barn. Ah when had the tables turned and which direction was she going to make a run for?

Barn fires were few and far between but she had this installed. When the bulls were young she would take them through so when they were older it was easy for them. And they showed the younger ones, though it was rarely used since it came out the front and not the back.

The mamas must have told them to go out the back and not the front. But that was only the males. The females were in a different section. No need of unwanted pregnancies here or of a few fun loving young male bulls getting out of hand.

Pop called her crazy but Gemma knew that if it saved her herd it was well worth the trouble. Easy in - Easy out. Walk them through a few times and they had it memorized.

But the animals never moved out the front to get loose, they would turn and enter the fenced area. Mosey around and do their thing. Get to the hay bales or water trough….

Well they did when Gemma or Pops had not opened the big doors to let them into the fields behind the barn. Again, the males on one side, females on the other and a nice tall strong steel fencing in between.

Gemma now pointed towards the house, "Can we go inside?" She was getting chilled standing there and figured that these guys were probably frozen. Broad naked chests with hard nipples. Yup they were *feeling the cold.*

'Don't look down, don't look down. Kilts don't necessarily mean that these guys were, are naked under there.'

OK, she looked down. Then up, green eyes met brown eyes.

The big man before her gave her a sharp nod.

So much for talking and heavy on the communication side….

Gemma took this as a yes and moved carefully towards the house. Passing the men and now, that she was closer, she saw that they were indeed covered in blood and other - stuff.

Uck.

She did her best to hide the fact that they stunk, no, they reeked. And they had been sniffing her?

The men whispered behind her but she did not look back. Moving carefully over the ground now getting icy once more she put her hand on the rail and went up the steps. Glad that they were not icy now.

Going up the porch, opening the door. Looking down and seeing Pops rifle leaned in the corner. She entered the mud room, turned on the lights so they could see their way in. Knowing that they were right - behind - her.

She heard noise, the men hushed. Maybe they had never seen a mud room? Was it different where they were from?

She took off her boots, hood, coat, both hats and hung them up.

Pulling off her scarf now because when in the barn she had been in a rush, she turned and watched the large men ducked as they now all came inside. Each looking around the space with wide eyes.

The room was quite large but now? Not so much.

Gemma had known the men were massive, but now, inside? They were MASSIVELY HUGE! The space shrunk considerably with them inside.

In her mind she kept repeating, *keep moving, keep moving* as she felt the room close in on her. She saw the space get tighter and tighter when they finally were all inside and stood there. Really tight…..

Going through another doorway, she entered the kitchen; again, turning on more lights. Hey, it was early, really early in the morning. She kept moving and hearing that the men followed. Again they grunted, made a noise.

Would she have to teach them communication? Why all the grunts? And they, well the grunts, sounded different. Ok, it was a guy thing. So Gemma let it go.

Here, there was more space. Open. The house was an open concept home from the beginning. Before someone called it *the Great room*. Greatgrandfather had wanted to see what was going on at all times. And no one that followed had changed much. New furniture or added family photos.

The kitchen with the small nook that held a small table for eating, now opened to the living room and the dining room to one side. Followed next was the living room.

The smell coming from the men was stronger now that they were in an enclosed space. There had to be something that she could do to get them to clean up. At least to remove whatever it was on them and Gemma did not mean the warpaint.

Good Lord was that guts on one man's boot?

Gemma looked at it then up the man's leg, finally settling on his face. Ok. He did not look happy that she did that but hell, this was her home and they all saw her take her boots off.

EWWW. Just gross.

Her mom loved sitting in her nook, and loved the view of the back yard. Now, the windows were dark due to the early hour. These windows did not face the side towards the barn. The overhang cut the light from the huge mercury lights. Shadows could be seen.

It was a view not often seen by Gemma, she would still be in bed….

Mom said she loved *'watching the world wake up'*. There was a glow from the huge lights, but here, it was shadowed by the mudroom that had been added on. Mom would sit here with her morning coffee and a smile on her face.

Gemma swallowed the memory. She felt her parents here still. The photos and nick-nacks. The memories. The…..

Gemma tried to keep the men moving.

Needing them to move. Not thinking of the mess as they moved. Whatever was or could be on their feet. UGH. She would have to do some heavy cleaning….

On her right was the stove, sink, fridge. Counter tops, central island with the stovetop insert and chairs surrounding it. Mom loved cooking and being able to converse with them at the same time.

Here, breakfast, well any meal was fun and shared.

All the wood floors, the walls where some had windows to let the day inside….

You could see the living room with the overstuffed furniture. The chair where she curled up to read…. Gemma blinked.

Why were these memories hitting her?

How often had she moved through here. Now she was seeing it in *their* eyes?

She could see the door to the den or office where Pops handled the paperwork, she worked there now. Here the files on each animal and every inch of the ranch was there, backed up on a disk now and stored. File cabinets held things, but disks were easier. On one wall was an aerial shot of the ranch when grandpa ran it. Next to that was one from just before mom passed. Not much of a change except for the forest. It was much thicker now.

To the side, at the front of the house were the stairs that led to the bedrooms upstairs.

The short hall to the large family room that grandpa had built. The fireplace he made with rocks from their river. This is where Gemma had the TV placed. The room was large enough for guests and even had a mini-bar sat up.

Gemma stopped moving. Something hard, solid ran into her, then huge hands on her arms so she didn't fall forward. Keeping her from landing on her knees or face planting on the once clean floor.

He grunted.

Gemma felt a warmth hit her from his hands. Wow. Why was she reacting to him like this?

Gemma got her barings then turned and stepped away, "You know my name, will you tell me yours?" She looked up and up. Gads how tall are these guys? She saw the strong face and the dark eyes as he looked down at her. It was the one man that had taken a step away from the others when they were in a circle.

The man still touching her now pulled his hands back, looked down at his hands and frowned. Looked at her and spoke, his accent strong, "Fearghas." He tapped his chest. Pointed and the others said their names when the digit aimed at them. "Kon-chur. Barra. Branhubh. Drostan." His accent was pure Scot. Thick. Strong.

But Gemma understood it. Odd.

And again that voice sent a shiver though her. Yes, odd indeed. She would need to call her BFF and find out if *this* was normal. Just a man's voice that could do this. Conjur all these feelings.

She stared into his deep brown eyes, her heart racing. How was this man making her heart react like this? He did not smile, not exactly, but now since he was inside he was more … more human?

She was a girl. A woman rancher. One who had not looked for a male to *take care of her.*. She handled things just fine herself. Pop had been gone now two years and not once had she asked for help.

OK. She lied.

She asked for help to transport the bulls but only because she could not leave the ranch with pregnant Brahmas. And now?

Now she wakes up and has five men appear out of a fog? Five men dressed strangely and acting as if they have no idea of what is going on?

Yes Gemma.

Your world as you knew it has changed.

Fearghas been so close that when the Lass stopped he ran into her. He reached out instinctively to keep her from falling. She was such a small frail thing. After nearly striping off all her clothing in front of him and his men she had simply walked away.

No word, just left. As they had no extra covering, they followed.

Stepping inside the next room as they made entry. Nearly turning sideways through the small door. It was a surprise to what was held inside. This lodge must house a king or queen. The items they saw, the wood and a real floor. Ceilings, though not tall, were also there with wood.

All this was meant for lordships and ladies. Not for them.

He nor his men were heathens, but they were plain and simple men.

Curious they moved to follow the female who smelled nice. Her stocking feet, not making a sound on the floor. Their eyes looked around and they stayed close together. Was this real?

The Lass said, 'this is the mud room,' But as I looked, I saw no mud.

The next room she called 'kitchen'. Kitchen I understood as I had seen many in my youth. But not one looked like this. There was no hole in the floor or wall for fire. No grating, no soot on the walls. Another odd thing. My brain was getting full of my *list* inside.

When the Lass stopped, Fearghas did not know that he had been that close and he nearly fell on her. Not his place to flatten the poor thing he reached out. Stopping her fall but then….

In touching her, he felt a change come over him.

As when the lightning brought them here, and lightning allowed them to understand each other, however this lightning was different.

It went up from his fingertips directly to his brain.

He inhaled again and his brain and body made a connection - to her.

It was direct. It was sudden.

His body warmed and he knew. Knew that he was hers and she was his. It hit him and, he understood, he knew he now needed her to understand…...

Fearghas spoke slowly as his eyes moved, searching her home, "Our lodges are wood and dirt. Long." He stretched his arms out, one hand smacked a wall and he jerked it back.

He eyed the wall, saw the men also look from the wall to his hand and back. Not one spoke.

Gemma smiled as she saw surprise in his eyes as he looked at his hand and the wall, though she did not understand why he looked at the wall so oddly. Her gut registered this fact but she continued. Wanting one thing, to get rid of the smell.

"You may want to clean up." She pointed at them. And again looked at their feet.

They looked at each other now. One or two frowned, another tilted his head and yes, she heard another grunt. Grunts would have to be interpreted when she knew them better.

Better?

Did this mean they would stay? That she had decided somewhere between the outside and here that they were staying and she would not be calling 911 in a panic? Ahhh. Now it was Gemma's turn to frown as she turned and made her way to the stairs that led up to a bathroom. A much larger bathroom.

Yes there was mud and other 'stuff' on them. Also on their kilts and their boots.

Two grunted. Again.

Gemma rolled her eyes, looked at the ceiling and blinked.

Fearghas had been watching her and saw her look up, so he did and saw, nothing but a ceiling. Were her lips moving?

As each of them sniffed. Yes, they needed to be removed of the fight, the blood and the sweat. Again they wondered about their wounds, all the injuries they had received were gone, cleared up. Or close to being healed. The deeper ones were taking longer and may scar.

But it was very odd that it was happening at all.

Healing.

They looked at each other as they moved around. Examining wounds that no longer bled. Looking at each other's arms, backs, chests. The places where blood now crusted but the skin, the skin had healed. Pink though bruised.

They moved huge shoulders as they flexed. Then they put their weapons in their sheaths and looked at each other, checking wounds and not finding any.

Blood, yes but no injuries. Seeing fresh skin where damage had been.

Odd.

They looked at Gemma and around them.

Witch?

No. It had to have been the portal. They had not been touched by anyone or any thing when they *landed* here in this strange land. And, they knew, this was a strange land. A place where a female walked with a strange beast. And lived in a lodge full of wealth.

This female had no sulfur smell, the lodge smelled clean. Not one thing signaled them as of her being a witch or crone. Or a conjueror of any kind. But, they would stay aware. Trickery abounds.

Gemma thought of the small bathroom behind them. The half bath that sat just off the kitchen to the side of the mud room. No, that would not work. A tight fit when there was just one, but for someone their size?

Wait - A - Minute.
Lodge? Dirt? He said lodge.
Did they *know* about running water?

Chapter 12

Gemma was told time and time again that she DID NOT have a poker face. And she now saw these men looking at her. A big hand touched her again, this time gently on her shoulder, "Lady Gemma, do not fear us. We will nay cause you harm." Fearghas said.

Fearghas decided that if this Lass lived like this, she was indeed a lady of the manor. And he and his men would respect her and her home. Calling her Lady Gemma was only one way to show her how he felt. And seeing her face light up, it was worth it.

She smiled, "I need to show you my bathroom and how it works."

She saw the face frown, nod, then in a moment he looked back at the men, "a bathing room she said." They nodded.

Turning back to her he said, "A bathing room and inside, indeed but you must have great wealth." Fearghas smiled as he looked down at her. His teeth were white in his tanned face showing out with his fullips and short beard.

Gemma smiled, seeing his reaction, studying his strong face and saw his eyes taking everything in. And now she turned and led the way, followed by a team of fierce warriors, as they trouped up the stairs. Stairs wide enough for two to move easily, but with these guys?

The stairs were built strong and had lasted for years, today, a few groaned from the weight on them. Gemma winced and silently prayed that no one fell through. The place was four generations old.

They entered a hall and she pointed when she opened a door. A full size bathroom. This was gonna be interesting. If they understood half of it, she would be thrilled.

Fearghas had seen the female, though strangely dressed, she came outside the lodge alone and without a weapon. She moved beside a large beast of a bull. Fearghas sensed somehow that she would not cause harm to him or his men.

He did not know why.

Then he understood her speech after that last flash of lightning. The one that was followed by the tremor that nearly dropped him on his arse because at the time, he and his brothers had been weak. They still were but would keep up with the small female.

Things were happening here that were indeed different.

Things that <u>he</u> did not understand.

But, he was the leader of his men and they would follow him. He could learn and if necessary, he would fight.

So far, no other warriors showed up. An oddity indeed.

There was no smell of others here.

No sounds of fighting and he could no longer smell the blood and fear that he had left behind.

This was due to the portal.

This place was here, he was here.

He and his brothers were safe - for now.

There was always the chance they could all leave.

And the chance that the portal would open and the English bastards would follow.

Coming here had been sudden, and just as sudden, it could all end. No one wanted to become swallowed up and find themselves in a very bad place.

Here, he felt safe and now was warm.

Here he and his brothers were healed from the fighting. Another thing to question.

This place, this lodge was strongly built. His eyes had wandered as they moved.

He did not want to leave, at least not immediately.

This lodge was unfamiliar but it was warm and comforting. The seating that he could see, had padding of some kind on them.

He was drawn to here and very drawn to the female who lived here.

But again the female touched the wall and the room lit up. When he touched the wall, nothing happened. Fearghas had felt something for this female and his hope now was that she was <u>not</u> a witch.
His men would never allow her to live…..
Was this place now no longer safe?
Was it a realm beside his realm?
Witch - warlock - sorceress? Or something else?
Was this female something that would harm them all?
And when they all inhaled again - she wiggled her little nose and squinted. Did she not trust them?

For now, he would keep her as safe as he could. She was small, delicate. She had no male to lean on. Protect her. A giant beast in another lodge that was free to wander but -
He needed to understand this world he had entered. His brothers depended on him.
She spoke in softness, not riddles or scorn.
Her face smiled at them and when she was thinking, it showed. She was not a witch. Nor she was someone that would cause harm. But again, she was not a simpleton and … she was alone.
Questions and no answers.
She did not make demands on him or his men.
She gave no commands. But?
If she is a witch…….

They stopped, heads turned and necks stretched as they all tried to see inside. The door, yet another small one that led into the room. He remembered homes. The wealthy had homes, homes and servants. Homes with doors and other rooms.
His head turned, and he listened.

No one was here other than them.

Large doorways in lodges were for men of height and bulk. Lord, some even could fit a horse if need be! Yea he had seen a drunk enter a lodge on horseback.

Fearghas, a man who had led his men in battle on many fields.

A fight or two in a tavern or two.

Worked their way through villages, farms, and many, many ale houses.

Found women who would laugh at their jokes and bring tankards of ale.

Women who would, for a coin, make you forget your worries for a moment.

But this?

This female lived alone. She did not dress to show her chest. She did not dress to show an ankle. Nae. She was wearing pants but she was covered.

No warriors lived inside or near, men protecting her. Protect her, her stock, or her land.

No staff supporting her.

Her friend was a beast who lived in what she called a barn. Where the yard was alight with things she called lights that looked like moons but were too close and too bright to be a moon.

He and his brothers had moved and not felt any 'wards' that would be used to hold back ancient spirits or bad things. The air now smelt good. Clear. And even inside these walls he felt, he felt something. Felt that here he belonged? Why?

They looked at the walls. Not one held a weapon. The floors were all hard, made with wood. The walls had windows and not one opening for shooting from. Large glass plates and ner one was soot covered from years of smoke.

Aye, Fearghas could see from the floors and a beam that this lodge was nae newly built but had withstood many seasons.

She, this small thing named Gemma, had a home, a lodge, with floors not dirt . Wood and what looked like glass in the walls. He had seen glass on his travels. Homes of the wealthy. Homes that were also well guarded.

Where were her guards? Servants, maids, cooks, those who cleaned and handled the inside for a wealthy female such as she was.

So many questions he needed to ask. Not that he was shy to confront her, but he wanted the right time to do it.

The large bull was like a puppy around her.

Her area had three moons that she called lights.

She - lived - alone. And as of yet not one had seen a weapon. No one had seen her glow. Wave her hands or cast one spell. Nae. Was she to relax them before the attack? Was she on the English bastards side?

Yes he and his brothers inhaled. Trickery at times held a smell.

They had watched as Gemma entered her lodge and moved her hand and the room became bright. She removed several pieces of outer clothing. And he was shocked as it came off, but not all, then she stood. In pants of all things.

And then moved, she knew this place she called home. And her hand would touch and light up the area. Take the dark away with her hand. No torch was seen.

She did that again to another room.

But he did not smell witch on her.

She smelled of flowers, not of strange brews. He had not yet seen a fire or a pot. No small animals hung on the pristine walls.

Then again, Fearghas had not met that many witches in his lifetime. He had been told of them. One had been pointed out. But becoming this close? Surely she would have an odor of something but, he did notice she smelled fresh. Clean.

The last lightning flash had him and his men now understanding her speech.

Was the Gods telling him something?

And now, more odd things.

The battlefield was gone. He and his men were safe here but, *where is here?* Here it was cold. Cold but quiet. As he and his men did not have their furs to drape over them they were not protected from the cold. Standing in nothing but their kilts and bare chests, they had felt the cold.

Now inside. Warmth hit them.

But he did not see a fire. Nor could he smell a fire. He looked, searched and found nothing that would hold the heat that he was feeling.

Knowing that even his brothers looked. Looked for the heat source.

Her offer was gracious. He and his men were welcomed inside and instantly felt the heat when they entered. Heads swivled as they moved. Taking in all that they saw and smelled. This and that and dark to light. Cold to warm. All of it, they saw, and watched.

But seeing the area, not fully open as what they were used to seeing.

Floors. Hard wood not hard packed earth.

Areas in sections. Like an ale house.

An area for sitting and eating, stairs that would lead to sleeping areas? Road houses had areas sectioned up stairs for sleeping. He understood but preferred to sleep under the stars. He, when traveling, had blankets and things. These items had been left with a woman in the village when they left to fight.

She, Lady Gemma, called it a home and not a lodge.

Sitting things that he understood, but these, these looked different. Nothing large for large men. But also not small for a child or female.

Separations. Walls.

Table, but small and the glass? Lots of glass **in** the walls. He wondered what he would see when the sun arose. Not one slit for fighting with arrow or spear. What kind of lodge is this?

Would their understanding be better in the morn?

He was tired and was sure that his brothers were also. The fighting had been taking their strength. But now. It was as if it was another day and they had slept. Was that due to the portal also? Still, he was bone tired, wanting to sit, rest and have a drink if he could.

This was a grand home or small castle. He looked back at his men, his brothers, and watched them all quietly observe. He knew that they would all talk later. They sniffed but did not touch.

Knew now that Lady Gemma saw them put their noses in the air and so they needed to be more subtle at it. Hide it from her.

Confusion but then again not.

A nod here, a look there.

They saw everything.

And now he knew why he saw Gemma's little nose twitch. Yes, standing here in this hall he and his men had a smell. Blood. Guts. Mud. Sweat.

Hell. And blast it all. They had been fighting for their lives and the lives of the village nearby.

His head swam. Fearghas wanted to lean against the wall but stayed upright. Things hitting him causing more confusion.

Where was he?

What country is this? Are there English around the corner waiting? Beyond the light outdoors? He had seen trees, were they beyond those, camping?

Here. Even he did not know if the walls of the lodge were safe. He had seen her touch and give the room light. No torch hung on the wall. No candle held in her hand. The light came from high. Inside the ceiling. Bright and not flickering as a flame would do.

So when his hand hit the wall, he wondered what would happen, but nothing changed. Odd.

Now here.

A bathing room. Inside the lodge. Strange or was it for the wealthy. The wealthy were weak and would stay indoors for winter. Use chamber pots that others would empty.

They stood outside the door and watched.

Showing respect for the female owner.

If not a witch, may she be a royal?

Then, where were her guards?

Her staff?

Chapter 13

The men all were full of grime. They had not truly bathed in over a week. They had traveled at a near run to get to the village. Finding what they did saddened their hearts. An earlier raid had left several homes burnt to the ground. Stock ran off. Crops ruined. Men maimed.

A nearby Clan had come in and pushed the English back. But not stopped them. Knowing that they would return and now everyone talked. Pledged to fight. To stop the English from entering.

Fearghas had taken his brothers aside. Taken a vote then they all moved to talk with the elders and had given their word that they would fight. There was no celebration, no happy faces to be seen from the doorways of those that they passed on their way out of the small village.

It was not even a mile to the edge of the wood. To where the land stretched out and you could see the gentle slope that was now between them and the English. To see the men, the encampment. The smoke from their fires.

Several guards stayed to watch. For a warning cry if the English came down the hill from their side. Or if they circled around to sneak attack.

At dawn. Fearghas, Kon-chur, Barra, Drostan and Brarhubh drank water and ate stale bread. Stood, stretched and removed their shirts and extras to stow in a pouch and left at a hut as instructed to do. Placing their swords in their sheaths that lay across their backs, a small sword in another, a dagger in their boot. They turned and joined the men facing the forest. Each gave a nod, turned and moved.

A full day moved by, fighting slowed but ne'r stopped.

A stench from the moors.

The smell of death.

Death that they caused. Now but a memory. He had not thought of what he left behind in that small pouch in a small home back in Scotland somewhere.

A look down and he even saw the stains on his clothing and also his booted feet.

Yes. A bathing would be welcomed.

Barra turned in the hall. His belted sword swung, a tiny table tilted, he moved quickly and settled it back on its four tiny legs, his hands nearly bigger than the table. Looking up at the faces that turned to him, his face reddened.

Not one made a joke of his clumsiness and the man relaxed.

Yes. What Fearghas told her was true.

She, this female did not need to fear them.

These men who voted to have Fearghas lead them, Kon-chur was his first in command. This was the way. They would heed his wishes.

They had all followed. The five lived together as brothers. They traveled together near and far and fought together. Side-by-side. Laughed together as brothers. Fought together as they would to protect the other.

Worked together and handled what came up. Anything that was questioned, they discussed over the campfire or in a huddle.

They had traveled to where the fighting was being done. Upon hearing the stories from those they passed on the roads, they wanted to fight. Fight for these people to be able to return to their homes.

First the battle, next was the portal, and now - here. Not knowing where *here* was had them all wondering. But, if they waited, the search would be over. The questions would be answered. The how and the why will always be asked. Soon, soon.

Fearghas led them and now? Now that they were up the stairs and watching the smiling female named Lady Gemma point into the room, the dark room. Nothing could be seen.

They saw her move, turn and again touch the wall.

Light. This time they did not jerk at the room suddenly lighting up.

The room was not large but they recognized one thing.

The tub.

This <u>was</u> a bathing room. And this caused several to smile.

So, curious now, they craned their necks and looked around. Then gasped and backed up when Gemma, who was inside, did something and … there was running water.

Smiling, she turned to them, "This is the sink. Here you can wash." She turned the water on and off, turned and opened a cupboard. Pulled out small and large cloths. She sat them on the area beside the 'sink'.

She turned and said, "*toilet.*"

She did something and again the men jumped, those that had entered and were closer now were scrambling back to the hallway.

"Oh shit!" Gemma said, "Sorry, you are used to pits or out buildings or even maybe using a pot. I am sorry."

She heard whispering.

Witch?

She blanched.

Gemma turned slowly, looked at them, really, really looked at them. Waited until all five were looking at her. Five big strong men. One could snap her like a twig. But she raised Brahmas, she knew how to stand, how to project a face that got attention and would keep you listening.

She had dealt with a stubborn calf that was twice her size and thought that a head buttt was fun. Or one that liked to step back so a hoof landed on her boot. And each and everyone she handled.

Now, looking at these men, she used that strength. She - would - handle - these - guys.

"Oh, no! I am not a witch. OK. Listen." Gemma calmed her voice and spoke, she wrung her hands together as she talked then stopped. Remembering that this she had to handle or everything will certainly go to hell in a handbasket for her. And she remembered her cell phone was downstairs in her kitchen.

OK. Time for the '*I will handle this*' face. No hand wringing allowed.

"This place where you are now?" She pointed at the floor. Watched them. Saw them look at the floor.

"It is different, but trust me, I am **not** a witch." She looked at the guys, pointed to Kon-chur, he was the biggest man and closest to her. "What year is it for you?"

Kon-chur looked at Fearghas who stood near the sink, Fearghas nodded that it was ok to speak. "The year of 12 and 17." He answered. His voice deep and it echoed in the bathroom.

Gemma's eyes widened, but she only said, "today, here, it is the year of 20 and 15"

She waited as they looked at each other. Gave them time to absorb what she just said.

"You have time traveled. This," she moved her hand slowly around her, "this is only some of the things that we have now. Now to have running water *inside*. To have a bathing room *inside*. And the other things that I will show you." Gemma did not speak slow but spoke clearly.

She looked at them. Knew that if they did not understand then they would deem her a witch and … they killed witches. She knew that. Scared of unknowns.

And with five of them and one of her. Well she could not even hold back one.

No more EasyPeasy.

She was alone.

And right now? Damn where was a big bull when you needed one?

She had to get them to trust her, really, really trust her. Because two were inside and three were outside of the room. Even if they were all in the hall her bathroom door would not stand up to them if they shoved it once.

She would need to show and explain lots of things.

She would need them to trust her.

But first things first, moving with care, she got a washcloth and ran it under the running water. She rung out the water and then put the cloth to her face. Turning, she looked at them.

They had to do something. The longer she stood by them the more horrible they smelled. And she was not going to ask what was on them other than blood.

There was something on a boot she was sure was guts. She had seen entrails when she got her first deer.

She did her best not to shiver. At 5'7 she was only up to one man's chest.

They watched her but not one pulled his knife.

Gemma took a deep breath. She said, "I will fix some food. I am sure you are hungry." She moved forward to leave the room.

The men backed up. Not one raised a hand to her or looked as if he would attack. They gave her space, moved.

One hit the wall in the hallway and jerked himself away.

What was it about the walls? She blinked. She would shelve that for later.

She smiled, passed them and went back down the stairs. Wondering if she should open a few windows to air out the house. She could smell them still downstairs. She shook her head as she moved back to the kitchen area.

Smiling when she heard the water come on.

Then off.

Then on.

She knew that they would figure things out. As long as they quit thinking she was a witch!

Chapter 14

The fridge showed that she had eggs and bacon and other things. Her head thought of five, count them, five **huge** guys with huge appetites…. OK. What do guys from the 12th century eat?

Should she google it? She eyed her cell, grabbed it and shoved it into her back pocket. She did not plan on leaving it behind again. Nope.

She had not prepared for company this weekend. She had gone shopping but had most things frozen…..

She moved again to get the cell and turn it back on, off the mute. Did not see any messages, yet. The missed call had been from Tyler, probably checking in but he did not leave a message so she let it go.

Time was not on her side here.

They would finish and be back down the stairs….

She heard a crash, frowned. Shook her head knowing that she could fix it later. Followed by a louder grunt. Then the toilet flushed and she gave a soft laugh. They were learning. It was like turning toddlers loose and ….

Ya, keep thinking of them as toddlers and she will make it through.

All 6' something, brawy toddlers.

Those men were men.

Those chests and legs and arms…

WOW but they had huge arms. Thick necks. Long hair that did not take their appeal away. Not one sissy was there. And there were their beards. Different shapes and types. One had no beard and it made him look like the youngest. Hummm.

The bathroom she could clean and mop later. She only had to resist running back up there to check on them. Right now she needed to feed a mass of muscular men. Men who would be hungry. It was 5:30 the sun would be up soon and it would be another day.

Thinking of Pop and how he would have enjoyed this encounter. Time travelers. WOW. Her Pop would know what to do and how to act. He would have welcomed these guys and showed them around.
 Man things. Pop would have took them out on a horse and ....
 Gemma was not a man and neither was one nearby, oh a phone call would have one here. But...
 But Gemma was at a loss here. Sure, she remembered her history. But this was nothing compared to a chapter in a book when she was in high school. Nope. Or from a movie or TV show of Scot's in kilts.
 And now was not the time to call Scott and wake his ass up to ask questions. History buff or not. Teacher or not. She may or may not fill him in and - alot depends on **if** these men stayed.

Gemma stopped moving and looked up. The rock. Stone-Mas. Did the rock do something? Turning slowly Gemma faced north. Thinking. She had been inside the barn when the lightning flashed. The brahmas had not acted differently. The air had been charged when the lightning struck. The hair on her arms stood on end.
 But vibrations? She had felt nothing.
 She heard the bacon crackle. Her attention returned and she shook it off and worked on breakfast.

Getting a large bowl she cracked eggs into it. Moving to the shelves she got the largest flat pan she had. A Texas sheet cake pan with high sides. Mom had two. County fairs and get-togethers and all. A family here needed things like that. Cooking for barn raising. Cooking for a new baby or a wedding. Church pot-lucks.
 This should work.
 She sprayed it well with grease and then pulled out the bacon. Cutting it in chunks she got it ready. Grabbing a few green peppers and seasoning she started making the largest egg / bacon dish that she ever made.

Scooping the bacon, give it all a stir.

She poured on the eggs with chives, green peppers and popped it into the oven.

Coffee?

Did they drink coffee? Well she did so she made a pot and poured it into a carafe. If that worked She would not need it, yup definitely needed it as she started another pot. It was early enough that she needed the coffee to stay awake.

Toast? Ok, just have bread. That would save the hassle of running to the toaster even though it was a 4-slice.

Looking at the clock she saw it was 5:45 am. She had been up just over 3 ½ hours. No wonder she was a bit loopy. Stopping, she listened. Hearing noise from upstairs she knew then that this was not all a dream.

She could call Scott. He was a history teacher, would he be able to help? It was Sunday, no school. But Gemma understood that *this* and *these men* she needed to keep secret for now.

Kinda like Stone-Mas.

Scott knew of the stone. All her friends had heard the stories Pop would tell.

But to explain this?

Even she did not understand **this.**

Then another thing hit her. Sunday. Today. Now. Well crap…..

Chapter 15

The men stood, looked at each other then at the room. A sink, a tub and the *unknown thing*. One said chamber pot. They looked at it again. Nodded. Now all faced the tub.

One turned a knob at the tub. Water ran. He jumped back, bumping into another, and they all moved, first away then - a chain of men now moved forward, closer. One hand out, the water heated….

Water ran into the tub and heads turned and smiled. Never one to pass up a bath, they moved again schucking everything. Metal, clothing, boots hit the floor. Bodies, now naked, Barra moved, stepped in and smiled at everyone. Water splashed his ankles, his legs and... he turned.

All was well until his elbow hit something and then - then the ceiling rained.

We, of course, knew it was a shower. But these men? No.

Heads moved, bodies moved as Barra barreled himself out of the tub as fast as he could move! The shower curtain jerked, tangled around him and he fell.

The men stood and watched. Looked at the tub, looked at the ceiling and at each other.

Nothing else happened but water kept coming down from the ceiling.

A hand reached out, then another and soon the men who were all naked and now they were clamoring into the tub, taking turns stepping under the stream of water. Somehow, the temperature adjustments were good as no one got scalded.

Gemma heard more water, was that the tub? They turned it on, but did they know how to plug it or to.... Gemma headed for the stairs. The tub would not overflow unless someone closed it.

Going up she stopped halfway when a naked man stepped into the hall. He was looking back into the bathroom and waved a hand. Smiling and wiggling he stepped further into the hall.

Happy and grinning and......

Gemma blinked, swallowed and totally forgot her name.

Dripping wet but he held a towel the size of, oh gosh, that was a hand towel?

Gemma looked up at the ceiling then down, closed her eyes saying, *'sweet baby Jesus'*, she should have showed them the full size towels....

Then another adonis stepped out, a huge smile on his face and also dripping water. Did they wash each other? Were they leaving like that? What the hell was their plan?

Why the hell did she care?

Was that the shower?

How had they turned on the shower?

Gemma's brain was coming back on-board and she moved.

She dashed past them, going further down the hall, opened the hall closet and grabbed the **big** towels. Thinking the bigger the better. OK, several big ones were beach towels but right now? She didn't care. Just wanted the men covered so she could...

Could not turn beet red.

Could think and speak coherently.

Ok, that was her plan......

Gemma looked at the men in their smiling faces, doing her best not to look at.... Or even look down and pass them towels. Then dashed inside the room to shut off the shower then the tub so it did not run over.

Straightening up she saw smiling dripping faces, hair and beards, big large white teeth (what did these guys eat?) on tanned faces. Happy men and now, clean men and breathed again doing her best to keep her eyes up and, huh.

Seeing that they were now wrapped in towels.

Yes.

Their heads were all wet. Did they dunk their heads? Chests dripping.

Right, the shower.

And how <u>did </u>they start the shower? OK. That question would wait for another time. They most likely don't know how they did it, but they did. Looking back at the men and the dripping mess of her bathroom.

Knowing that her face was red she wanted to stick her head out of a window into the winter air. She stood there and saw men who were happy. Not a bad thing.

Hearing the timer go off in the kitchen she said, "Breakfast, down stairs."

She turned and moved. Blessing that stupid timer.

Not remembering who she bumped, passed, touched, as she tried her best to not look at those healthy, naked specimens that stood there.

GAH! Those chests. Never had she seen pecs like those.

Those biceps, thighs and legs.

And the memory of someone's tight ass…

Ok, several male butts.

All male, no doubt about it.

And mercy sakes, no tan line. Not a one. Her memory stored it for later. She wanted to giggle all the way down the steps, she held it in and chewed her lip.

Well not that she had seen a naked man before. Nearly naked, in a bathing suit but all naked. No. Not really.

And she was blinking, chewing her lip more and surprised to find herself back in the kitchen……

Chapter 16

Getting the casserole out, the smell filled the kitchen. She moved back a step to place the huge pan on the stove, that done she backed up into - a chest. Firm and now it smelled soapy clean. For once Gemma was glad she used 'regular' soap in the guest bathroom, keeping the flower scent for hers.

Not that many stayed over and showered. Guests since Pop passed were few and far between. Even her mother's sister had not been over in years. They would talk on the phone. Keep in touch.

Her instinct told her who it was without turning.

Fearghas. The one that stayed close to her before.

Which was just fine for her. Something was *there*. A chemistry between the two. And Gemma liked it. But to put it into words? No not ready.

Chemistry or not, she did not know what to do next. Should she make a move? Does he make a move? Will she let him make a move?

This means a nice long talk with her BFF.

Again, huge hands held her steady, she took a deep breath. She said, well maybe she squeaked, "Plates," and pointed up when she sat the large pan down so her hands were free.

He moved, stretched and opened the door Gemma had pointed to, pulled out plates and sat them down.

Eyes sparkled as they watched her.

"Thank you." She wanted to look elsewhere as she feared that he was not dressed but saw color. A beach towel with colorful buckets on it. The towels that she got for Tyler's kids when they visited and everyone went to the river.

OK The man was covered. Barely, but covered.

Gemma looked up and around and saw all the men were covered. The towels were suitable, it covered them the same as the kilts did. They now had long bare legs and bare feet.

And still lots of bare chests.

OK. She would work with that. The parts that *needed* to be covered, were covered.

Just needed to inhale and exhale.

Not look at the skin in front of her, concentrate on the food and it will all be over.

'*Yup*', she spoke to herself.

A few chests had lots of hair, another's not so much but all were muscular.

All chests were built for fitness magazine ads.

WOW. The ripples of chests, abs and those bulky shoulders? Their hair was still wet but not dripping any longer. Towels hung past their knees, around their slim hips. Twisted and fixed, or so Gemma hoped, to not fall off when moving.

Hell, their kilts were wrapped, the same with a towel, right? Well right, if the towel was large enough. And there the thought of buying bath sheets hit her. Something she would be goggling and ordering later so this would not happen again…..

Again?

Gemma saw the breakfast nook, looked at the men then said, "moving to the dining room." Not paying attention to them looking from one to the other. Possibly not knowing the word or thinking she used small tables only.

They watched her as she pointed and moved, then as she moved to another room and they followed. Going around the corner she waved her hand like a game show host so their attention was now on the table itself. The big table with all the leaves in it and the 10 chairs because Pop liked it that way. Four would sit on the sides, one on each end. Big, wood and solid.

She smiled, showed them the table, pointed to the chairs and turned.

Again hitting Fearghas as she ran smack dab into him. She face planted into his chest because she turned suddenly.

A nice thing? "Excuse me, I need to…" As she stepped back, bounced back, depending on who saw what happened. Ok, she bounced back off him.

Fearghas stepped back. He inhaled deeply and smiled down at her.
Gemma saw that chest flex right - in - front - of - her.
Did he just sniff her?
She saw then that he had taken two towels and tied them together to cover him. One now draped his chest and over one shoulder. As a kilt would. Huh.
She blushed.
He smiled.
She dashed into the kitchen.

A tray. Now plates. Silverware. Cups. She plunked the coffee carafe in the center. Grabbed the tray and looked behind her, no one was there. Whew. She turned and moved to the dining room.
She sat everything down. Turned and left. Grabbed the bread and butter. Came back to the dining room and blinked. The guys had not moved. They stood beside the chairs.
"Please sit." She said. Not a command, a request. Softly spoken.
They looked at Fearghas, he nodded, they moved.
This is when Gemma's mind remembered that they always looked to Fearghas, OK. He was their leader. Good to know. The men sat on the sides, not in any of the end chairs.

Gemma filled the cups with coffee and sat them around, then left. Leaving them to use the sugar and cremer if they wanted. She returned with the casserole and again stopped. No one had touched anything but - they had sat down.
OK.
She put the big dish down, at the end of the table, plated the food to get it out.
Again, no one moved. "You lift your hand, take the plate, please." She knew who to look at, Fearghas.
Fearghas did hold out his hand. She handed him his plate, then he sat the plate down in front of him. Gemma plated the others and passed them out as each man lifted his hand to receive it.

That went well.

Fearaghus had watched his brothers earlier as they washed. They smiled at the warm water. Then they had to stop it. The tub was fun. No one wanted to sit in it but they took turns dunking their heads under the water and small towels into it.

When the roof rained on them, it was another grand experience. Behold a waterfall that was inside and it was warm!

Then the soap. Not the same as he had been used to. Something not harsh nor was it flowery. But it still worked. And it bubbled. Grand. He never had a soap bubble before. It made him smile and it did wonders on his and the other's hair.

They took turns and washed each other's hair, laughed and they looked happier. Felt better and knew this, whatever it was, was a good thing.

They checked each other's wounds, and found that all were healed or healing. Nothing needed stitches. Good. Kon-chur carefully checked Fearghas's head injury and grunted it was ok. But badly bruised.

Fearghas was glad, a headache was worth it not to have a bad injury. His dizziness was gone until he was near Lady Gemma. But, he knew it was not the same thing. This was no injury that caused it.

No one had spoken much yet about the predicament that they were in. Fearghas figured he had time to figure things out. Soon they would be alone to sit and talk. A plan was needed. One. To find where they were, what country and how to move about to get from place to place.

Two. Find a village near, look for their people.

Three. Find the English where they were hiding.

And....

Hearing footsteps he knew it was Gemma who appeared up the stairs, looked at everyone then moved again to another door. Now everyone had a larger towel to surround them. Not that they were bothered being naked but he saw by Lady Gemma's face that it bothered her.

And this was her lodge. Being covered was proper.

He remembered again, she lived alone.

Had she never seen a man? Would he be allowed to ask that question?

And when she moved, she flew. He nearly hurt his neck to keep his eyes on her. She also knew where everything in her lodge was located. An oddity in his mind. People of status had others do things. Yes they were not simpletons but they were respected and had *helpers* to do these simple things *for* them.

Fearghas had seen this time and again as he wandered. Learning as he traveled and watched others. Those of wealth and those that had only love and family. People had more when they had love and family, that he was sure of.

But alone. This female. All by herself here.

He did not understand that.

Not one serving Lad or Lass to help her.

And from what he had seen from the windows, no lodge was nearby. A lodge where a worker or servant lived.

The smell of breakfast as she called it was good. Breaking fast was good for them as it had been several days since they last ate a meal. A dry piece of bread was his last memory of food. That and water from a nearby stream.

Going down the stairs from the bathing room he got a better look around. There was wood everywhere. Doorways, arches. Nothing very high up for a ceiling but that also explained the stairs and the other level that was above his head. Was there another above that?

He would get a better look when the sun rose.

Looking side to side, seeing things that he was not familiar with. It bothered him slightly. He did not understand that, but he felt safe. The strange smells and sounds now comforted him. Her lodge was clean and he had not *felt* anything hanging in the shadows that were few but still there.

The lodge felt open and airy but held doors. Doors closed could hold many things. Sooner or later one of them would be checking, looking. Not because of being curious but for each other's safety.

The thought of the English attacking was in the past even though it was but a few hours ago that he nearly fell from being tired.

He had a memory from traveling. The portal that moved him and his men also moved his brain. Parts were returning and he would remember the rest after resting.

Several taverns had sleeping areas above that they rented rooms out. Some had a bed or a pallet on the floor. Possibly Gemma's lodge had places to sleep up those stairs. Did she lodge others here?

He had not smelled another. So the answer to that was no.

The sun was coming up and the many windows now showed much land and nothing else. Sunlight hitting the snow and reflecting. Shadows lifting. Nothing would be hiding in the light shining as it awoke everything outside as he viewed it while moving.

She lived alone and away from others? No other buildings could be seen from here. From the windows he looked out in every direction and not one more lodge could he see other than the one with her cattle.

He would ask her later. Where was a nearby village and how far was it to a clansman's house. This they all would need to know. Find the Clan and let them know that they were here and on their land. Get permission to stay, if would be allowed.

So many things that needed to be done.....

Find the Clan leader and talk. Find this before they found him and his brothers and either fought with them or forced them to leave.

Fearghas wanted to stay. Wanted to learn more about this woman. Lady Gemma.

He reached the floor and felt refreshed. Good.

As it was, with his height and that of the others, the ceiling was low enough to touch if he wanted to. He hid the urge to reach up and kept his arms down. But he smiled from the thought.

He smiled. Another thing he and his brothers had not done in some time. But up there in the water everyone smiled and also there was laughter.

He liked the softness of the colorful clothing that he was using. Knowing now that his brothers were down here waiting for him he followed his nose to where she was and again she was busy attending to him and his men.

Sniffing the air more this time, he did not smell another.

Again. She is alone.

He did not understand.

All this wealth and not one maid? Not even a young lad to help with the cattle?

She was small, this Lady Gemma. And she did not question him or his brothers other than to get the year from them. He had been as shocked as the men all were when she said they were in the future.

How was this true?

But seeing what he was seeing, he had to believe it didn't he? To believe her and hope that it was true and that she was not a witch. He would be happy.

To be away from the fighting was good, but now the question was, who won?

Being close to her, he felt comfort. Something no other female made him feel. And he had known lots of females in his 5 and 20 years of life. His first when he was but 6 and 10. She had been older and showed him the ways. He had enjoyed her and also those that came later.

Never settled down. Always moving.

He would hear his mother's voice of her wanting a grandbabe on her lap to hug and to nurture. He would smile at her and shake his head no. Now, she was gone. Was everything too late?

But now? Now he was interested.

Very interested. And, it made him smile.

They all had moved down the stairs, barefoot and in their colorful clothing that Gemma called 'towels'. The sun was coming up and the sky was changing colors. Brightness glowed outside from the snow on the ground.

Snow.

Where were they?

The valley he fought in was green, not white.

His eyes looking out showed mountains. That may explain some but not all.

Finding Lady Gemma was simple. Not just his nose but a string.

No. A rope that pulled him to her.

He watched her as his men moved about as they looked at things. Not one reached out to touch what was hers unless granted permission. And, as of yet, none had spoken. Made conversation. Not that they were shy, but still confused and searching first so questions would follow.

<u>And</u> they all stayed away from the walls.

Watching her move around the area and the smell of food. He knew his stomach was empty as those of his brothers.

Fearghas got closer and closer. Feeling the pull, wanting to touch her. Before she was so covered he could see parts of her face. Then when she came inside her lodge and pulled clothing off and she became a tiny person.

Slim.

Her hair pulled into a 'thing' that held it high and it moved like a horse's tail.

He was mesmerized by her. He never had these feelings about a female before. A sensation of wanting his hands on her skin. Wanting to hold her and see those green eyes look up, for him, wide and open and…..

He nearly said loving.

Seeing her slim neck since her hair was up. Again odd. Women covered their necks. Covered their legs, nearly covered their feet. Showing a dainty ankle could cause talk. Seeing a throat bare was scandalous. Having her hair up and on her head, was what Ladies did. But not women who worked besides husbands in the fields.

Lady Gemma had said the year was 2015. A different time. A different word. Truly, something would tell him if this was all true or not.

Her lodge was indeed different. An animal he had not seen before was different, had he and his brother time traveled? Traveled into the future?

He felt a tremor run through him as he suddenly stopped and bent when she did. Surprising even himself that he was this close to her yet again.

Lady Gemma bent and pulled something out from a hot area. A tray from a fire pit? Like a cook in yon kitchen? He felt the heat but did not see any flames. She closed a door of metal, sat the tray down and stepped back, she again bumped him as he was still bent to look for a flame.

Her soft voice, the smell of flowers, those green eyes…..

Eyes not showing any fear of him or his brothers. Also not looking wicked or trying to be alluring. Lady Gemma did none of those things.

His mama said, *'love is like lightning. When it is there you have to grab it before it is gone.'*

His memory shook him. Lighting.

There had been lightning than the portal…....

Gemma said 'plates', she pointed. He understood. He understood her language. He remembered the first time she spoke. He had not understood it then, and again, there was lightning and after that they all understood one another.

Another question filed for later to discuss with his brothers.

He knew what a plate was, also called a trencher as what he was used to using. Something to eat off. He had sat in long halls full of men. Trenchers full of food would be sat before them and they would eat and talk. Maybe listen to another talk from a near table.

Everyone had their own knife or dirk to cut the meat, another utensil for softer foods when needed were placed with the trencher or found somewhere on the long table where they sat.

Fearghas liked the sound of her soft speech. She smiled often Fearghas noticed and he was happy to see it. When she turned and saw his brothers, she frowned and said, 'Lets move to the dining room'.

Was something wrong?

They followed her like puppies to this *room for dining*.

He too had seen the small table and bench. Knew that maybe one, possibly two could sit comfortably there. But not all of them. And even though he had stood to eat many times, this was Lady Gemma's lodge and if she moved them, they would move.

She stopped and showed them the large table and chairs, pointed and told them to sit. Not one bench but individual seating places.

Fearghas felt all their eyes look at him. This was odd to them.

Yes, the chief or elder would move to sit first but here? There was no raised stand with another table. Only one in this space. Then the chief or elder would be served.

Here Gemma was the chief.

This was her lodge.

The owner of the lodge would sit first and be served first.

This. There were no servers, no maids, no workers.

They waited.

Lady Gemma came back and gave orders again to sit. So now they sat. She moved back to her kitchen and came back. Looked at them and bit her lip.

He thought she looked, what had his mama said, sweet? Was that the word women liked? Fearghas was not acquainted with women's feelings. A bar wench would nearly jump into his lap.

That, he understood. He would have his time with one, and it was over.

Gemma. Lady Gemma was different. His treatment of her would be different. But he would only move to take what was granted.

She stood, got things on the plates and handed one out when she told them to hold up their hand. She served him first.

Did this mean?

Did she understand that this showed that she <u>chose</u> him?

This pleased him greatly.

His chest swelled at the thought. He had to fight his grin. He was proud that his brothers moved then to take a plate from her hand and also that they waited for her to sit and eat first.

He knew that they looked upon him and he felt their feelings. Happy for him and that of him being chosen by Lady Gemma.

He smelled the bacon but the rest was different. He looked at Lady Gemma who now sat, pulled her plate forward, took a forkful and started eating.

Everyone followed. They ate.

Egg. He recognized the taste but not the look. Fluffy and melted in his mouth. It did not run over and get caught in his beard. He was happy to eat this food. Also to pass the bread that was already sliced.

Saw Gemma use the butter with an odd knife and they followed suit. Also using the tiny silver things as they watched her use them. A very blunt knife that would ne'r cut a slice of meat but did well to put butter on the bread.

Fork and knife a utensil, but these were much smaller than what they were used to. The men did not use their fingers to eat anything other than to hold the bread. Fearghas was proud of their manners. Knowing that they were trying. Holding back behavior they thought she would see as rude.

She sipped her coffee. They did also. No gulping. No slurping. The only sounds heard was of everyone eating. A fork on a plate.

The drink, it was hot and she would pour more coffee when one man was finished. They learned from watching and soon served themselves. Not wanting her to wait on them. To show that they could learn and also be useful.

It was a different brew but it warmed him. Not bitter or burnt taste.

Stronger than tea but as he sipped, Fearghas liked it.

Lady Gemma smiled as she watched the men eat, soon there was nothing left in the large pan and she again smiled at them all. Like a mother proud of her family that she had cooked for.

His family.

His chest again warmed. She accepted him and his brothers into her lodge and now, possibly more. He liked the fact that this Lady Gemma treated *them* as family. But not wanting to be treated or though of as a child. Her smile as she looked at them as if happy she fed them and happy that they were there to share in her bounty.

But.

They were men.

Warriors.

Someone burped, she giggled.

His heart filled. All was well in his world right now.

She accepted them. It was good.

They all took notice that she had not frowned when they moved wrong or did something that got her attention. No. She would look, but smile and they were all relieved.

Kon-chur had watched her like a hawk.

That was his job. His job was to protect Fearghas and was there to insure no harm came to their leader. And now Kon-chur had looked at Fearghas and nodded. He accepted the Lady. Was also letting it be known that he did not fear her to cause them harm.

Fearghas was glad.

Fearghas remembered the soap he used and Lady Gemma had left it for them. Another good thing. He sat and watched his brothers who conversed softly between themselves and Gemma sipped her drink and looked content. Relaxing in her chair.

This he would like to continue.

To be here like this, a family.

Could he make it so? Could he stay here as well as his brothers? With a barn and cattle there was work. Although they had only seen one beast, there were others inside the nearby lodge, he and his brothers could smell them. And a horse or two were there also.

He could now see a field beyond the window. Yes, it is snow covered but where there is cattle, there are hides. With leather available, they could make clothing.

Clothing for boots or for other coverings.

If they stayed.

They understood metals and how to work with that. They could forge more spears, swords, anything that was needed for work or a fight if needed.

They understood leather and bear along with deer hides.

Antlers make good handles for knives.

The animal hooves make strong objects also.

They could find ways to make work for themselves, if they stayed. And if needed, they would fight. They were warriors.

The sun sparkled brightly off the snow. Windows of glass were nice. The glass allowed them to see and not be cold. The rooms were warm and as of yet not one had seen a fire pit. Odd.

A fan moved as it hung from the ceiling. Warm air moved about them, keeping him and his brothers comfortable even though they were not actually dressed.

Kon-chur had made a pass earlier, quietly moving through the lodge when he got up from the large table once. Upon his return he looked quiet. Fearghas saw that as a good thing. The man's eyes would flicker with worry if something was wrong. And all would then be on alert.

Fearghas sat, stayed quiet as he drank more coffee. From his seat he could see far in the distance as he looked out. Seeing a fenced in area and soon several large animals moved about, routing through the new snow looking for grass. Again, these were the huge bulls similar to the one that Lady Gemma had with her.

Lady Gemma made a noise and stood upon seeing them. "I need to check them. Can't believe I forgot."

Everyone stood, alert. As they would stand for their chieftain or queen.

Them? Who was *them*?

Was there danger? They reached for their weapons and eyes darted toward the stairs where swords and knives still laid on a floor above them.

She moved, standing, looked back, "You guys relax." Then she left the room. The men still stood. Relax? A new word.

Everyone sniffed the air and listened.

Chapter 17

Fearghas had heard stories when he was a lad. Women who were warriors and lived alone. Also of witches and fairies who lived alone because a man was not needed. Or another version would be where the warrior killed any male that got in her way, a tribe of Amazons. Where a man would be taken and used as a stud for several to keep their lininage going. Also of where witches bound a male to a place to be used over and over.

And he remembered these were from the women folk when he was very young. And it followed with *'stay close to home,'* when he wanted to follow an older lad or his da. He had his friends would talk and say that they would show a woman a good and rightly stud if one was a'looking.

He looked around. Here he felt safe and secure and knew his brothers were here, also warm and safe. Lady Gemma had not once made them feel not needed, instead she had welcomed them into her lodge and had shared food with them all. Not making any move to cause harm. She had not once raised her voice or her hand. (And they all looked to see if she yielded magic. If in her fingers or hands.)

She had not given commands or looked upon them oddly. Nae, she was kind and he sensed that this was na an act of any kind to entice him or the others to do a wrong.

He saw na one weapon in any search. Nothing was visual other than a rifle in what she called a mud room. At most lodges, weapons were proudly displayed. Hung on walls to show strength and craftsmanship. Easily grabbed if needed. And everyone wore at least one. Women had underthings that held small daggers.

Here, he had not seen one. Noting that there was a block of wood that held knives of shapes that upon inspection thought to be used for cooking or eating. At stops or taverns, even barns or a lean-to, there were weapons. The land was harsh. Animals roamed, not all had four legs. From looking at her, he knew she had no weapons on her body.

This lodge smelled *safe*. No odd odors of sulfur or a pot boiling on a fire. Of witch or of fairy. Of something that would trap him and his brothers. They felt no wards to stop them from moving around while inside. As for the outside, not one had ventured yet.

No smell of another male or animal inside.

For these reasons, Fearghas relaxed more and more. If indeed this was a trap of some kind, he was learning to enjoy this *trap*. She had water inside that was warm and she also had walls that when you touched them, would light up the room. He would find the trick to that one soon. It was rather odd that only she could produce the light.

Kon-chur looked at Fearghas after licking his plate clean, "What do you make of this? This is true? We are in the future?" He looked around. The others nodded and also looked at Fearghas for answers.

Fearghas sat up and looked at his brothers, he was truthful in his words, "This is unknown to me. I canna answer something I nae nothing about. We need to give it time. If, if this is a trap of some making, we will all stay alert and on guard."

The men looked, listened then nodded in agreement. They would wait and be on guard for any trap. Eyes wandered toward the walls that no one trusted yet. Of the shelves that held things.

Of the yon glass that now brought in light so they could see better. There was no haze of smoke from a fire burning to keep the place warm. And, they would again search. If their eyes didna see, surly their noses would find it.

Kon-chur looked towards the stairs, Fearghas knew it was because their weapons were up there. Being that he had been the last to come down and knew they were left on the floor above them along with their dirty clothing.

"I doon na understand that this woman is alone. Surely there is a male for her, a guardian or elder to watch over her?" That came from Barra.

Drostan stood and looked around, rubbing his arms and smiled. "I am inside, I am pleased."

Now everyone stood, moving the chairs back as they moved and looked around. Chairs made noise on the wood. The brothers looked around them and moved closer, inspecting. Aye, wood on the floor. Walls that were dark from the wood coloring but at a soft glow from age or from being taken care of.

The lady of the house took care with her belongings. Not one trap door in the flooring had been found.

The walls surrounding them held shelves with objects and photos. People smiled back from the photos and the objects were fine looking and colorful. Paintings, they had seen but these were small, delicate. Yes, that was the word, delicate.

The table, though not overly large from their point of view, held single chairs and not a bench. There was not a large chair in front of the one fireplace that they had found. No dias. This would be where a chieftain would sit, or the elder of a clan. Here? Still no one stepped out other than the Lady Gemma.

The window in the wall was quite large, larger than they had seen before.

And the glare now coming off the snow....

The coldness did not enter the room.

Again there were questions that he held. Needed to ask at another time. But surely there were places where one stood to shoot at those that attacked. Did this place stay hidden near to trees?

The men nodded as they also looked around and all sniffed the air. "It is odd, truly. I am as confused as you. We watch and we will learn. If needed I am sure there will be another portal we can find so we can return."

This made them all quiet. Looking at each other. Did they want to return? Would it be back and in the heat of battle? Is this what they wanted? To return to fighting?

Or did they think as he did?

To stay here.

There was no fighting here that he knew of.

It was a good feeling not to worry.
To feel safe for even a short time was pleasurable.

War. Bloodshed. It was not a life they were looking for. The smell of food cooking, a lovely woman's smile. A soft bed to lay in. A lodge that was warm. This was a good thing.

They had no family to speak of back where they came from. They had each other and would follow or fight together as brothers. They had clan connections, they needed that to move about and not chased. Not treated as rogues and threatened. One could find a sword or pistol in one's face if ye hand no connections.

Fought to keep the English off their lands. Working alongside other Clans. Mentioning the one that they were from. The Lairds granted them access to cross the land to get to their home that was farther north.

Hearing of the English bastards that came. They moved as one to go and fight. Again asking for access to cross the land to fight with the clans there.

Worked hard to keep the women and children safe. Free-born men and women, some had small clans backing them up. Some lived beside a strong clan, not being of one but of many.

But would fight to keep their lands safe. Push the English back. To stay aware was to stay alive.

Gemma popped around the corner, and they jumped. Covered again as she was before when they first saw her, with only her face showing "I will be outside in the barn. Need to take care of my cattle."

She looked at the faces watching her. "You will be ok left alone?"

The men nodded back and she smiled. She was ready to leave then she jumped. An unknown sound, musical notes filled the air. The men looked around as they still stood....

Her phone rang.

She had turned it back on when she planned to step outside, then ran back to check the guys. Remembering that they did not know where she was going. So used to being alone.

Men moved, stood, suddenly alert.

Men checking for the sound, for danger.

Gemma moved from the dining room as she pulled her phone, "It's ok, I got it." She waved her hand with the *thing* now in it and still making a noise, ignoring them now when she saw it was Freddie.

"Hey kiddo! How's everything?" She spoke into her hand holding the square.

The men watched as Gemma moved away.

Gemma moved quickly through the kitchen, the mudroom and out the door. Knowing that the phone spooked the men. She had not thought to explain the phone to them, well, it was not as important as getting them out of their grubby clothes, and now she had her brahmas to take care of.

"Did your generators kick in? Are the little Brahma mama's ok?"

Gemma had to laugh at her friend, "Yes my power is fine here. Had a bit of a jump earlier, but from what I have now? I am back up and running fine." Gemma paced on the wide porch as she talked. Squinting from the glare coming off the snow.

"Well, if mine stays out we may be moving everything to your place. My generator won't hold running everything for the house. I put all my money into the barn generators. Guess I need to upgrade the house one.

"Also Scott has a dinky TV and yours is at least a 60". And your family room is huge enough …."

Gemma turned in a full circle on the porch and saw the men, faces now pressed against the glass watching her through the window in the door. They were inside, still all toweled up but still….

She turned away from them and faced the barn. Crossing fingers that their hearing was not super powerful. Not that the conversation was private but still….

She must have made a noise….

"Gemma, <u>what</u> is going on?"

Freddie could always catch Gemma in a lie. So how do you tell your bestie that five, count them, five, nearly naked men are inside her house? Not exactly a normal happenstance in <u>her</u> life.

"Something has come up Freddie and…."

"Oh hell no! This is <u>the</u> SuperBowl. I need a TV and I <u>need</u> a party!" Freddie practically growled into the phone.

"Ummmm." Gemma ducked her head, closed her eyes and….

"Gemma. Spill it. You can tell me anything, you know that." Now Freddie's voice got quiet. Maybe sensing that something was wrong.

Gemma turned now to the faces watching her. Turned her back to them again and started talking as she leaned against the post on the porch. "You won't believe me." She closed her eyes remembering this morning. Was it only a few hours ago that her small world turned upside down?

"Gemma?" Freddie said with a bit of worry in her voice.

"OK, OK. Sit down."

"I need to sit?"

"Sit or no story."

"OK. I'm sitting. Just remember my phone's battery life, ok?"

Gemma started, "This morning the clock showed 2:02 then my lights went out……" When she was done telling Freddie what happened, it was quiet. Gemma looked down at her phone but Freddie's pic was still there. "Ahh, Freddie?"

"No Shit?"

"No shit, I swear," Gemma said.

"5?"

"5."

"Why?"

"What?" Gemma asked.

"Why you?," then she gasped, "It was that damn rock wasn't it! I'm coming over!"

"That's what I think too, my problem is, well right now, ummm, they need clothes."

"Clothes? Why? Oh hell don't tell me they showed up buck naked!"

Gemma fought a giggle, "No, they showed up dressed. Kilts actually. But now they are in towels. Bath sheets and beach towels. Kinda colorful actually." Gemma turned to the guys and gave them a smile. Then turned away again.

Freddie snorted, "Oh hell yes! This I gotta see! Take a pic and send it!"

"Wait! No!" Gemma got quiet and said, "OK, you can come but I gotta find clothes for these guys. And they are like, huge! I have no doubt that they are all over 6' tall. And their chests…."

"Give me time to get there and we will put our heads together." Freddie was still laughing. "Did your dad leave any sweatpants or work clothes behind?"

"No. I gave things to the Church …." Then Gemma smiled, "I can get stuff from the Church! Can't believe I didn't think of that!"

Freddie said, "I will come over. Get some measurements. Get my phone charged while I am there and together we will handle it." She hung up. Gemma looked and saw Fearghas now standing there.

Beside her again. Here, on her porch.

He had another towel but this one draped more over his chest and shoulders Not like she had an extra coat here for him to slip into. Did he take one off….? <u>Not</u> going there. Not even going to turn and look. If someone was missing their towel now… Her face went red.

Fearghas had surprised her by being so close. He looked down at her, should he tell her that he and the others heard her talk to the black square she held in her small hand? That their hearing was excellent?

That they knew she talked about them?

And that he could *feel* her worry?

"I have a friend coming over." She watched him.

He looked at her then her hand. Still not understanding how *that* gave another voice in the air but no body or form was visible. He had to investigate, that is why he came outside. But could not smell another person. But he could hear a female voice…

His brothers had whispered 'witch' again.

"We are a problem. We can leave." His strong features were softening as he watched her. He felt bad, his brothers and he were a problem, too much for her to handle. They had eaten, maybe she did not have many supplies. The men could eat their weight if they wanted to.

Yes. She was alone.

Yes she was far away from another lodge. He had looked when he stepped outside. Not seeing anything but the one lodge for her animals and this one. There were trees and a wide area that would hold fields when the snow was gone. This was all hers? She was the full owner?

But leaving? Where would they go and how could he leave her when all he wanted to do was hold her. He inhaled again, this woman, this Gemma filled his senses. He could not leave her.....

Or if he did, it would not be far. Maybe to the animal lodge that she called a barn.

Gemma shook her head and waved the hand with the little black thing in it. "No. My friend, another girl, woman, she's ok to come over. We will get you some clothes and I will get your stuff washed.

"I said that I have power, she said I can have the party here.

"She said I have power and a big TV,..."

She gulped. "Oh ding, dang, dammit. I am having the SuperBowl party here at my house!"

Gemma turned and waved her hand in the air again the hand with the black thing.

Fearghas moved to her. He now felt - knew that she needed him.

He hugged her. "Calm down little one." Wrapping his arms around her in her bulky outerware'. Her size was not a problem to him. His arms held her and again, his world tilted on its axis.

He was glad that now he held her. He liked it, holding her in his arms felt right. His chest swelled, or it was his heart, he did not care. He had her and that was all that mattered. Her scent filled his nose and he wanted to inhale as much of her as he could.

"How do I explain you guys to everyone? Kilts. Swords. Oh hell, I need to hide your weapons so no one gets hurt. But the guys, the party." She looked up at him. Her thoughts bouncing back and forth.

"We made it this far and no blood was shed." His eyes twinkled looking down at her. Seeing her once wide eyed look calm now.

"You promise?" She giggled as she relaxed into his arms. Why it felt ok she did not know, but hey, as long as it works, she was content. This was actually the first time that a man, a real man other than Pops had held her.

She liked it.

"I promise." He still held her. He felt her relaxing in his arms. His chin now rested on her head. The sensation was new to him but he was finding that every - single - minute was worth it.

The sun was warming him and he barely felt the chill as he held her. He would tell the men that another female was coming and that she was a friend of Gemma's. The discussion of more people coming would wait.

First find out how their reaction would be with Gemma's friend. A female friend.

Fearghas knew that his brothers understood that this little one was interested in him and that he was interested in her.

They all witnessed her feeding him first. That she <u>chose</u> him.

And now, to see them touching.

It was a bold move and she had not slapped him for being forward. To be so bold with a maiden would cast her in shame. If another found out that he was this close, or would speak so frankly with her and for not having a female near. A guard of some kind. Someone to shield her honor. Another female was arriving soon and Lady Gemma's honor would be safe.

She left his arms and the porch as she moved to go out to the barns to check the animals. They were fine and her guilt left her as she made sure the animals had their feed and had enough hay.

Double checking the water supply.

Next she checked the pregnant mothers. All was well. She left two extra buckets of water for the mommas and the pregnant ones. Young ones were still nursing and all needed to stay hydrated in this weather.

She would come back later to get the stalls cleaned then get showered for the party.

Party.

Oh please, don't let anyone get hurt.

Chapter 18

Faces turned. Men tensed. They waited for a signal from Fearghas. Saw the two on the porch and Branhubh thunked a large hand on Kur-chur's shoulder, "The lass has him tangled and wearing a towel. What is next?"

Kur-chur looked over his shoulder. "Be kind. She has the food and the lodge. If ye want to sleep with yon cattle, keep ye mouth open." Kon-chur turned to look back outside. "The towel covering my arse and is soft. Though I may like it, the color is not me."

Barra laughed, "Ye make a joke! Tis a long time gone since you last joked."

Now everyone was quiet. Acknowledging that right here and right now? They were warm, fed and safe. Yes, it had been a long time. They were lost in their thoughts when Fearghas returned.

The room where they stood held many odd things. Several were white. Two were similar and one tall standing one. Of course the men looked. Thinking the metal things held weapons or an oddity. But what they found was two that were empty and looked like a large tub of come kind. Gutless. The other was large and flat, upon lifting the lid it was as if they stepped outside and was full of colorful packages.

To touch one was icy on the fingers.

Nothing smelled.

Odd. An ice house_inside_ the lodge. Another wondrous future thing?

The men watched through the glass, took turns running around and returning. If they found something, they whispered amongst each other. But, nothing spectacular had been found, yet.

Fearghas entered, still smiling although now he had felt the chill hit him. He looked down at his bare feet and back up. An eyebrow raised as he looked around the room. Knowing his brothers had 'scouted' the place.

If anything was to be reported, they would share. But the faces before him? Not one looked excited. Knowledge was good, and not one knew how much time was on their side.

The knowledge of what had transpired hours ago was still fresh in their memories. Aye, they were here. In a lodge and warm. They had eaten but.... So many questions and no answers.

Fearghas let the worry go after seeing that nothing looked out of place and the men were not harmed. He had also seen the fire stick and had looked at Lady Gemma. She owned this? It was a new thing that he had only seen but a few times. But she did not carry it with her when she left her lodge. Thinking that she was safe when outside. Or knowing that she was safe outside. This *was* her land.

He talked now to tell them about another female, a friend of Lady Gemma that was coming. They looked around and moved back deeper into the lodge. As they were thinking of going up the stairs to retrieve their weapons, they heard a noise....

This, this was a **thing**.

A thing of noise, moving and coming closer. The wagon of sorts was without a horse or cow to pull it forward. It made noise that they had not heard before. A rumble that made the ground vibrate and their ears strained to place it.

They heard, listened, moved as one to a large window and stood alert and now watched as Gemma laughed as she ran from the lodge holding her cattle she had gone to and straight at the big metal noise maker.

Again, the men watched and waited. Windows were good, they could see everything from where they stood. But they could not smell or get closer. They would have to go back through to where they had just came. Another door near was unknown. They had seen several and one nearby held clothing and odd footwear.

They knew that Fearghas was smitten by the female that dressed oddly. She wore pants. Nothing was leather but a different material. And the colors, bright. Such as the clothing she had given them earlier after bathing.

She lived alone, could touch a wall and make the room bright. She did know how to cook. And the big cold thing in her 'kitchen' was just cold. They had looked and did not see anything they recognized. Boxes with pictures. Other boxes were clear. A drawer that held vegetables. Finding potatoes, onions and other foods.

The weird thing that held milk they found out as Barra drank from it. Confirming it was from a cow. They had quickly put things back and looked at other things.

This had been done while Gemma was outside talking to the air then she moved to the lodge holding animals. The fire pit she had used earlier was now cold and dark inside. They had opened it and looked inside, sniffed and closed the door.

Strange. They had found it in their search. Taking turns watching for Lady Gemma to return or for Fearghas to stop them. If he said stop, they would.

Quick in their actions and no sound from their bare feet.

Kon-chur stayed at the door and kept watch while they scattered and looked.

Drostan watched now while Fearghas was outside with Gemma while the others checked things quickly. Men moved, opened up doors and found shelves of boxes, or glass or more plates.

Kon-chur was as curious as the others. His height was a help with so many upper cabinets.

A strange thing with the plates from earlier on funny shelves.

Another in a low cabinet that spun when touched. Things boxed with writing and some pictures. Hard to tell the flour from the sugar unless you opened it and sniffed. This was from lidded jars on the counter. Needing to see the inside, a finger would scoop or touch and they would make a face. Finding flour, sugar, tea.

Again, they wanted to run up the stairs, so many doors to check behind, but there was no time. So, that would wait until later.

Running around barefoot was interesting and they liked it. It was warm where their feet touched and their feet stayed clean. The floor was wood and not hard packed earth. No splinter. The wood smooth from wear. Pleasing as their feet moved from room to room.

The towels that surrounded them, though pleasing, but were not proper clothing and they wanted their kilts. But right now? It was fun for them. Even childlike. And they found themselves smiling when watching each other. Aye the cloth did nae stay tight and would slip. They caught it before it hit the floor.

It had been so long since they had played a game like this. To run and search. Not to run and search for danger or a bad person. But this, this was gamelike. A door would be opened, a head would pop in, finding nothing of importance, they moved on.

Fearghas returned and said a visitor was coming and it was a friend of Lady Gemma.

Now? Now there was a metal thing moving to the road and then it stopped and got quiet. They reached to their sides for their weapons and came up with air. Their sword belts had been removed when they washed.

Heads turned towards the stairs, then back to the glass window they stood in front of. If needed, they knew that in a flash they would be armed. One stood at the foot of the stairs.

All focused on the metal thing and Lady Gemma as she moved towards it with no fear or weapon.

Freddie got out and hugged Gemma then turned and saw…. Men. The wide window had men standing there looking out. Arms crossed their chests. Faces stoic.

Gemma had not been joking. There in Gemma's front window stood 5 men. All in towels. Bare chests, arms and legs. Some had facial hair and all had longer hair that covered their ears. One had long, dark hair held back by a leather band. One blonde, another with hair in ringlets. They stood, watching her and Gemma. Their arms crossed over their broad chests.

Freddie looked back at Gemma. Back up at the window to see the men. Not a photo in front of the glass but men. Eyes watching her. Eyes that made her squirm maybe a little. She had seen how men would look at her. She was not a 'shy girl' from the ranch nearby.

She, Freddie Meyer was a woman, a rancher and, she licked her lips and smiled, a single, hot-blooded female.

"Dayum Girl! You were **not** joking."

Gemma gave a laugh, "Just be nice and remember to watch what you say. They are from the 'old' country and don't understand a lot of things. And will take things quite literally if you catch my meaning. We say things one way and they hear it and understand it another. I am forever catching myself and have to think of how they are interpreting it."

The girls moved, arm in arm to the house. Gemma said a prayer as they moved. *No blood, no talk of war, no talk of being naked and not understanding the bathroom or….*

The men moved back from the window but watched the two get closer.

The 'front door' (that Lady Gemma called it) was opening and Gemma entered with the female behind her. This door the men had not opened earlier, the wood was different and, well, they wanted to have someone with them when trying an odd door. Now. They knew that this also led to the outside. Was there another?

No time to retrieve their weapons. No time to look like a male warrior.

And here was another female traveling alone. Another thought to be filed away for later to discuss. Men inhaled. Yes. A female and no, no male. Were all the men gone? Could that be why he and his brothers were sent?

This was getting difficult to fathom. Men traveled alone or even in pairs but females? Never. They looked back outside. Perhaps a male was waiting inside the metal thing? What kind of time were they inside of?

Gemma turned, "Freddie, these are the guys. Guys, this is Freddie."

Men's jaws now dropped when the female turned after stomping her boots from the snow and pulling her hat off.

Long blonde hair fell down around her shoulders and she smiled up at them all.

Her big blue eyes widened when she really looked from one man to another. Five men. Gemma had not joked with her. Big. No, *huge*. One blonde, two brunette and two black haired men looked back at her. Large and nothing boyish here. If Gemma had ordered the men as dancers, Freddie may consider these guys real.

But that was not the case. Gemma said that they *appeared with the fog* early this morning. How did it happen? Five men together, showing up at 2AM? The enormity of the situation was difficult to place in an analysis. Nothing came to mind that that was even close. *Time Travel*.

Freddie's mouth opened then closed. Time travel had to be real. This proved it. But - for how long? Would they just *go back* tomorrow at 2AM? Or would others show up? Is Gemma safe?

She blinked, looked at them from their bare toes to the tops of their heads. Turned to Gemma and said, "I honestly did not believe you."

Gemma laughed as she took Freddie's coat. "Told you so."

"Yes you did." Freddie stood there and looked at the guys, giving a little wave, "Hi. I am a friend. Gemma's friend."

Gemma snorted now. "They understand english. They aren't barbarians." Then she blushed. "I mean….."

Someone grunted, one growled. Both girls jumped.

Fearghas put his hand out, kind of to get attention, Gemma looked at him.

"Are we in England?" His voice was different; she picked that up immediately. As were his eyes, now serious, very serious. And one man was backing up and had a foot on the stairs. The stairs to their weapons lying on the bathroom floor.

Gemma clamped down on the shiver running through her and looked them all in the eyes and said carefully, "No. No, it is our language, English. You speak Scottish. Your accent is Scottish.

Here it is english but we are not in England. You were fighting the English, right?"

Here all the men nodded. "Aye," one of them said. Their faces were fierce. Muscles rippled as their stance hardened. Attack mode? Gemma did her best to stay calm and not panic. 'Panic never helped anyone' as her Pop would say.

"Freddie is here to help me with clothes for you all. We, here are Americans. Not British or English. You are safe here." How in the hell was she to get them to relax? To not run up the stairs and grab their stuff?

She had not thought that bringing her BFF here may endanger her.

"We have," Fearghas started as he looked towards the stairs. He was going to tell her that they had their own clothes. "Coverings." he finished.

"Right, I have to get those and clean them. But Freddie can help me to get you something else to wear while I wash your kilts. You know, pants and underwear…"

"Underwear? Like they have nothing under there?" Freddie pointed at the towels. Now, several mens heads looked at her, than the floor. Back up to her once more. But the fierce look was gone from their faces.

Gemma now relaxed and fought a giggle. Well that distraction worked. Got everyone thinking about clothes and not weapons. OK. Good.

"Well damn," Freddie said softly. She pulled her purse around and was fishing through it and pulled out the measuring tape and a notebook.

Eyes went up, watched her. Again they tensed.

"I can call Tyler. He will know where to find clothes for right now. Get these guys covered up and then Monday we go shopping!" Freddie said as she moved. Excitement in her eyes as she pulled out her stuff and laid the purse down on the floor.

"Ahh, no." Gemma said, shaking her head.

"Why not?" Freddie said as she moved now and stepped up close to Barra who was the closest to her, she smiled and pulled the tape in her hands around his waist. Was going to say something but the man she had a hold of, jumped back as if electrocuted, then stood still and looked down at her, her hands holding the tape, then back at the others.

Gemma moved and touched Freddie's arm pulling her back a step, "You need to ask before touching them." She said firmly. Now looking at the guys, "I am sorry that she touched you."

Freddie looked at Gemma then stepped back, looked up at Barra, smiled and said, "Can I touch you?"

Barra nodded now as he stood still, looked down at her and gave her a wink.

Freddie's blue eyes widened. "OK." She moved along with getting her measurements.

Gemma continued, "These guys are from out of town. Wayyyyy out of town. I am not shoving them into a metal can and driving to a store to try on clothes. Not gonna happen." Gemma was trying not to visualize the chaos of the men in one of their stores. Stores with others and seeing racks of clothes. From all she had read, clothing was made for the person to wear, not from a store or building that held clothes. Material, maybe. But ready made clothes? Nada.

She watched as Freddie made a note on her notebook. Watched Barra's face as he frowned at first then relaxed. But watched Freddie as she moved.

Freddie wrapped the tape go around Barra's chest then moved his arm to stick it out as she measured his arm length. The man looked down at her again frowning.

"And what is your name?" Freddie looked up at the man that she was touching.

"Barra," he said gruffly. His muscles rippled as she moved the tape. It tickled. He did his best not to wiggle or laugh. It was more difficult than he thought.

Freddie coughed, caught herself then said, "Barra, can you turn, I need your back, to measure shoulder to shoulder."

The man turned pink, red then looked around for help.

"Oh, they will get their turn." Freddie said innocently.

Now all the men looked at her than at the floor. Embarrassed? Gemma bit the inside of her cheek to not laugh at them.

She would hope that Freddie would ask first before touching another man, but if she did not, the poor guys were doing quite nicely considering.

A stranger just showing up and now touching them? Touching their skin? OK. This was one for the books. Skin on skin contact with a female was a no-no, right?

Fearghas moved, signaled Gemma and whispered, "outhouse, chamber pot?"

Gemma pointed up the stairs. No one moved. She looked at them again and tilted her head. "OK, everyone, up stairs, now."

Freddie looked at her, but didn't say a word as she made her notes. But was intrigued that when Gemma gave an order, the big guys followed. Huh. Interesting.

Gemma went up stairs and the towled men followed and Freddie followed behind everyone. Getting up there, Gemma stepped inside the bathroom, picked up the kilts off the floor, kicked the boots to one side and then stood in front of the toilet located on the other side of the sink.

She waited until she saw the now guys watching.

Then she said, "toilet. Outhouse or pit, or chamber pot, It is _inside_. This is what you do with _my_ bathing room." She stood, turned her back to the seat. Pretended to pull her pants down and sat. Leaned, pulled some paper off the roll, 'wiped' and released the paper into the bowl. Stood, turned and flushed.

Again she pretended to pull her pants up. Moved to sink, washed her hands and dried them on the hanging towel.

Gemma turned to them. "Do I repeat it or do you understand?"

The guys grunted, nodded, looked at the toilet then at her.

Gemma looked at each face.

"OK then," and Gemma left the room. She stopped and turned. "One man at a time. And you _will_ wash your hands when finished, promise me."

They nodded and she went down the stairs followed by Freddie. Before reaching the bottom step they heard the toilet flush.

Gemma inhaled, "Toddlers, I need to think of toddlers," she closed her eyes and took a deep breath.

Freddie laughed, "Instructions for the bathroom? Priceless." Freddie hugged Gemma around her shoulders, "I'm here for you," but she was laughing. "And as for inseam measurements, I will make a guess on that one."

Both girls then laughed. Yes, getting measurements of anyone's inseam would be a bit overboard right now. These men are going through a lot of information getting thrown at them. Measurements would have to be quick and hopefully painless for the four men left.

Gemma now had her arms full of towels, wash cloths and kilts and several odd pieces that she tossed upon a flat sheet she had lid on the bathroom floor so she could haul it all. She wrinkled her nose at the stench but kept moving towards the mudroom, dragging it behind her. Leaving Freddie in the kitchen to plug in her cell. And sit at the table jotting notes on the guys stuff.

The men were *exploring.*

She knew it and let them go.

Knowing this was all new and the need to know where they were and if, if there was anything here that could harm them was huge. Afterall, they had been in battle not 12 hours ago. A nasty battle from what Gemma was finding on their clothes.

Gemma looked at Freddie and saw that she was busy, Maybe she had no clue about the men moving around here on the lower level. As long as nothing got broken, Gemma was fine with the men snooping. Because soon, they would be in one area and there would be others here. Now Gemma did roll her eyes just thinking of these guys, 5 guys. And her friends all in the same room.

Dumping the sheet with its haul all on the floor she gave a sigh, "I never washed a bloody kilt before."

She picked one up. The thing was long and heavy. Not the 3'wide material she was used to handling but wider and long. Sheesh. How they wrapped them and got them to stay on was weird and Gemma knew that before they left they would show her…..

But now? No buttons, belts, nothing but material.

Left? Why would she think of them leaving? Putting her mind back into her work,

"Cold water I would say. No dryer. It has to be pure wool." Freddie offered some insight as she held her nose when she finally followed Gemma and saw the mess on one. "Maybe they should be washed twice?" She tilted her hand out but made no move to touch anything.

Gemma remembered a tidbit she had read once that Scots of old, would fight naked. To save on their clothing being ruined. But then she turned pink as it hit her and she questioned where that thought came from and how would she find out if it was valid or not.

Would the men answer her truthfully?

Oh nuts, why would they lie? There was nothing to gain if they told her an untruth. She could google it and find what was right and what was wrong.

Gemma nodded. The answer was not important now. Now she had to get their clothing cleaned and back on their bodies. She put the kilts in her large washer, glad that she had one that would hold the load. Mom said that she needed one to do the bed covers and Pop got her the largest model they sold.

Gemma shivered seeing the 'things' that were on them. She held them over the basket and scraped whatever it was off before putting it inside the machine. Shivered. "Yup. Two, maybe three washes." Filling the tub and pouring in the soap, she turned the dial to 'heavy duty' and 'full load'.

The washer started and Gemma got the towels and other things separated. One leather boot dropped down on the floor beside her, Freddie jerked back, "Is that what I think it is? She pointed at the offending boot.

Being ranchers, they had seen a lot of things. Gunk. Grease. Stains that made a woman cry. But this, this was serious and this was … Gemma closed her eyes.

Gemma looked at it, her voice low as she said, "They showed up covered in blood and stuff. I thought at first it was mud. But when I got close to them, I saw guts and … stuff. They came from the 12th Century Freddie. I am not kidding.

"They were in battle, an actual battle and somehow ended up here….." I look at my friend, blink and say, "they were killing the English who were burning and killing….."

Freddie looked at the boot then at Gemma, "They are the good guys, right?" she asked softly and checked over her shoulder.

"I hope so." Gemma said as she looked at her friend, the door behind her and the washer, "I really really hope so." She bent, pulled the plastic bag from the basket. Made a knot in it and and sat it just outside the door on the porch. She would take care of it when checking the cattle later. Get it out of the house, and soon off the porch. No need for a wolf or something to smell it and then bother the calves. There was definitely guts from someone there.

She shivered and looked around. Listened to the washer chug with its load and do the job it was supposed to do. Clean. She shook her head. Moved to go back inside.

Freddie had also heard Pops tell the story of the Stone-Mas and of Vikings, Warriors and time travelers. Scotland this and Scots men and of tales of old. Passed on from father to father.

The girls had sat up at nights around the campfire and looked into the sky, thinking of the wild tales. Men on horseback riding to help the women and children. They visualized and smiled before getting into their tent and sleeping. Even being 10' from the porch, camping outdoors was fun.

And now, Gemma possibly has these Warriors inside her home.

Freddie had got the rest of the measurements. Careful now and asking permission to touch the men. She had not thought earlier of 12th century men. But seeing the condition of their kilts made her think twice about touching or moving fast. She had seen the stuff on the bathroom floor.

Not one sword but several. Yuppers. Big pieces of steel. Just like in the movies.

Gemma said they had been in a battle then 'whoosh' they were here.

Freddie finally settled down and was not so skittish after getting the rest of the measurements. Then called Tyler and checked on the power problem. He said that lots of places were running generators and that Gemma was the only one with full working power that he knew of.

Service crews were in town and things were being handled there first before the ranches. Tyler had told the workers that many ranches had generators and that they were all working from the contacts he had made. That he had been in contact and also no one had been injured from the ice or the power being off.

Tyler said that Freddie's place was one that was still not powered up, or from what he was seeing coming in from the service men handling the work. But her place was on the list as it was not that far out. Hers and Gemma's were small and easy to get to.

Tyler said he would round up some clothes. Gemma had explained that she had out of town guests that lost their luggage.... He accepted that. So far, so good.

Freddie had plugged in her phone and checked messages. Sending texts about the change of venue for the party. Looked around at the hunks that filtered in and around the house.

Bare feet, no noise. Just look up and there one was, watching her. She would smile, make another note on her phone and try to ignore the bunch of muscles that they all had. They were sure moving around here inside, but that was not bothering Gemma so it did not bother her. Gemma probably gave them permission to look. That was what Gemma would do.

The urge to take a photo was great.

Then she remembered Gemma saying 12th Century. And that kind of corrected her brain. The thought of where they had come from and then remembering that they asked to use the outhouse. Outhouse? 12th Century.

Freddie looked up and again saw a body move by.......

The washer dinged. Gemma went out and checked. There were some that needed more scrubbing. She finished and restarted everything. But the boots were another story.

Told Freddie to watch the guys, Gemma dressed and went out to the barns. She needed to finish with that and worry about the guys later.

Freddie had seen Tyler when he made a quick stop after messaging her. He stopped for only a minute. Handed out several bags of clothing and left. She understood that he had his hands full in town and was checking the other ranchers. He wasn't the only cop on duty but he was working hard to keep everyone safe.

She had slid as she moved across the drive to get to his truck and back to the house. Stomped her feet and removed her boots and coat. Grabbing the bags she moved.

Took the clothes and dumped them on the couch. Separated them for the guys. Sweat pants mostly, but that would work. Using her notes she made piles.

T-shirts, hoodies. BVDs and socks. Everyone had something to put on and hopefully be comfortable. Better than a towel!

Chapter 19

Drostan nudged Barra when they stood looking down into the kitchen, "I like the new female." The men stood in the hall upstairs. Waiting their turn for the chamber pot that Gemma had named the toilet.

Barra stared at him. "I was the one she hugged first."

Kon-chur looked at them, "We are here wherever here is. They are nice females but let them choose. We cannot make enemies of them. I have nothing to keep me warm if I am removed from Lady Gemma's lodge." He looked at them, both squirmed as he then said, "You will be nice and not handle the females."

Drostan rolled his blue eyes, "We know Fearghas chose Lady Gemma and that she chose him. We can wait for Lady Gemma to bring more new friends."

Barra grumbled, "But I like *this* friend."

Kon-chur bumped his shoulder, "You want the yellow-haired bairn. Be patient." Then he looked down the stairs at the two women he could see at the smaller table, "and be nice."

He turned and he entered the bathing room. If Fearghas and Branhubh could do it, so could he.

Fearghas was downstairs now and taking his turn looking around. Sniffed and moved but noticed that Lady Gemma was gone. Her flower smell faded. He moved further into the lodge. He wanted one thing, the thing he could not find, namely the fair Gemma.

Finding the other female sitting at the small table with a dark thing in her hand like one Lady Gemma had and a drink sitting before her in a mug with a saying on it. Coffee, he smelled the brew.

Freddie did not look up but pointed at the door over her shoulder. "Gemma is out back. Her babies you know."

Fearghas frowned. He must have made a noise. Babies?

"Oh," Freddie looked up, "You *don't* know do you. Sorry. Those Brahmas' are her babies. All of them. She had coddled them since they were born. They think of her as their mama. Follow her like puppies. She needed to clean up….."

But Fearghas was gone. Freddie felt a slight breeze but that was all.

"OK, I can see where this is heading. One down now which leaves four to go….."

She smiled and went back to her phone, fingers flying as she texted. Getting everyone to know that all would be held here at Gemma's ranch. That she had no problem with her power or her phone, but not once did she mention the 5 extra guys.

What Tyler knew he already shared, she was sure of that. Not that men gossipped. What a joke, they were worse than girls!

Lady Gemma was not hard to find when Fearghas entered the lodge the female called a barn. Thankful that his feet were on something more solid and not slippery. Yea, the trek was slower paced as he was with feet bare.

The place was around 50 degrees so it was comfortable. His feet would thaw. He had stopped after entering and listened to her, a smile crossed his features as he listened, she sang as she worked.

Cleaning a stall, letting the large animal back in, cooing to him or her then moving to the next one. Seeing that the huge animals did not have closed gates. Some were in a large open area, the young ones not quite a year old, now this gate was closed. Keeping the babies safe.

Then a few that were separated because they were female. To stay away from the bulls. The bulls that watched him as he stood there. Big, strong and for some reason Fearghas did not fear them to charge him, but did watch with those big dark eyes.

Each and every animal got a pet and soft words. She turned to him, acknowledging him and put her finger to her lips. He followed and saw four large Brahma mothers with their little ones. This area or pen was larger and one mama turned a big head, watching him. Warm brown eyes, inquisitive but watched as he was a stranger.

He held still.

Gemma sang and moved, opening the gate and entered. The youngsters looked up and big ears flapped as they listened, scented her, three ran to her and one moved behind his mama.

They made noises and butted her with their heads.

Gemma laughed as she hugged them and petted them. Finally moving out she went to another section of the barn. Fearghas now noticed that the building was 'L' shaped he now found as he followed her. Here there were horses. Again she repeated her job cleaning the stalls.

Four horses of varying ages, one old one. Also Fearghas saw saddles, bridles and other hardware. He recognized most of it and again saw that Lady Gemma had much wealth. Again he wondered *where* all her help was.

Even a poor Queen had servants. Or at least a maid.

And here he was, watching as Gemma cleaned the stalls. Each and everyone of them. Gave love and attention to her stock. He also saw the way each animal looked at her and would be gentle back as she was gentle with them.

Understanding now what Lady Freddie has said, 'her babies.'

When he first heard, he had to shake himself. Why he thought of human babies and why would this kind woman have them kept somewhere different than her lodge

Seeing now as Gemma moved to the old horse and brushed him saying, "You handsome boy. I bet you want spring back as much as I do." She held out a chunk of carrot for him.

Not looking back but knowing that Fearghas was watching her, she spoke. "Pop has been gone for four years now. Jake here was his favorite but we have not ridden him for a long time."

A tear fell as she brushed the horse. Her hand soft as she brushed his coat.

"Why do we age?" She looked over at Fearghas.

"You, you stepped through time. But you are now the same age as you were yesterday. Some things never change. You are born. You grow up and you age then you die."

She hugged the old horse, patted him and let him back into his clean stall. Taking care of the brush and a few other things. As if trying to be busy as her mind was.

Fearghas waited, giving her time. The feelings hitting him he understood, but questioned. Why? He turned his head and looked around. Seeing things both familiar and unfamiliar.

Why this female and why now?

Was he sent *here* to find her?

Was she his destiny?

What had happened to them all out there on that field? He had been so close to collapsing and the portal opened and he had a burst of energy.

There was a powerful force that was drawing him closer and closer to her.

For some reason, when she smiled he felt warmth.

She looked at him and he felt as if there was sunshine on him.

He wanted to move, lay her down and claim her. He breathed deeply and looked at her, saw her look at his face and at his towel.

And it hit him. Here. Here he had nothing to give her. Even if he could take her back, there was nothing he owned. He had no land, only his name. He had respect from his men, brothers each one. But no home to take her.

He shook his head. Things were not looking up for him.

Gemma seemed surprised but not afraid.

Again he asked himself why.

If he was a female and five warriors appeared out of the sky, he knew he would faint, cry or wail. The men were large bruts and Gemma, Gemma was handling everything as if this were normal.

He scented her again.

She was feeling as he was, he was sure. She was not cowed, no. And seeing her with the big brutes of animals and them acting docile beside her. She had shared love and not a spell. Not a witch. But had feelings for all animals.

The men, his brothers were talking about him, he knew that.

But these feelings, he had them and all were real. This woman who allowed them to enter her lodge, eat her food. She cooked for them. Cleaned for them. And not once asked for anything in return.

No sly looks. No barter. None of that. She was not coy but at times shy.

Her movements were swift and she had not once reached out to touch any of them, but she allowed <u>him</u> to hold her.

What kind of world had they all stepped into? Was this what the future held? No more fighting? No bloodshed for land? No sneaky bastards coming to put fire on fields of grain. Burn simple homes. Take women and children for slaves, workers. To grab then slink back over the borders.

His thoughts wondered again as he looked at her. She was covered from head to toe but he knew what was underneath most of it. Inside her lodge, she would again remove the heavy outer garments. Her clothing, though not leathers, were colorful and drew his eyes to her curves. He did notice her small waist, hips and his eyes had noticed her bosom. Aye. He may be from the 12th Century but he knew a woman when he saw one.

Then his thoughts skittered, went elsewhere, he had seen several bales of hay, thought of removing his towel, nibbling on her skin as he removed....

Gemma turned, "I got these guys handled, I needed to see Jake last - as always."

Then she stopped, looked at the man staring at her with heavy eyes and could easily see his towel was now tented.

She blushed but he stepped closer and his dark eyes warmed as he moved closer, he was so quiet in his steps. And her mouth went dry. She looked from him to the hay where she had seen him looking, back to him and .....

Gemma looked up at him and felt - felt something. Then stopped.

One horse snorted, bringing her back. Making her thoughts clear.

"We need to go back inside. There is a lot to still explain….."

Fearghas stood there, inhaled, looked down at her. "Yea undo me. Lass, I try to catch my breath when ye be near to me. My head spins to watch you flit around. Yea show respect to me and my brothers and it pleases me greatly. And - and I need, nae, I want tae hold yea yea." His eyes looked deeply into hers, "Yea understand me Lass?"

Gemma's tongue was stuck to the roof on her mouth. Did he just proclaim love to her? He did. She knew he did. But they did not know each other. They had just met this morning. And what a hell of a morning it had been.

The stance he held, the look in his eyes. Soft yet determined. He was saying that he wanted her. Her, Gemma McWyntr. A female from today the 20th century and he was… Right. He was from before.

Gemma closed her eyes. She had to calm down and stay away from this man. He was dangerous to her heart. He was telling her things she wanted to hear but would he even be here tomorrow or the next day?

She cleared her mind, her hand reached out to him and touched his chest. "I need to have more time. I need to think. Do you understand?"

"Time. Aye." He nodded then smiled. His large warm hand cupped her cheek. "I will give you time Lass."

They turned then and they left the barns together. Stepping from the warmth of the barns to the cold, they moved across to the house and entered.

She had felt the change between them as they had been alone. Electric. She knew that if she followed through that no one would come outside to the barn to stop them. But with this all being so new. Not that she never dated but that she never, you know, did anything.

But now, with this man, she did want to.

But, would he and his brothers be here tomorrow or even next month?

Inside Freddie was eyeing the men now standing around in the living room. They were talking low and she bit her lip and tried not to laugh. They had all shown up to watch her sort the clothes and now waited. They looked down at the outfits, sweat pants. Pants were not normally worn in 12th Century Scotland.

Aye, men had worn pants, but these were unfamiliar to them. And the tops. Shirts with tiny sleeves? How could a man not have his arms covered with the cloth?

Unknown to Freddie was the fact that the men were wondering about her.

Another solitary female.

No escort.

Moving about on her own.

Not carrying weapons.

They had sniffed her and no male was scented. Also no animal.

They had looked at each other several times since meeting her. Was this a land of only females? Another question. But it seemed a male was available, one did hand over these bags to her. He stayed inside the metal noise maker then left.

And also the strange dress. Pants on females, they were not used to that.

They also did not wear pants. They had seen them. Leathers were worn by hunters mostly. Or a pant farmers wore while working the fields to keep the flies and chiggers off their legs. Nasty little bugs.

Odd. What clan was this?

The language they partially understood. Also odd. They would listen and learn.

And the way the two women interacted - friends not warriors. But when they spoke it was low and soft. Difficult to pick up the words.

Questions, lots of questions…....

Freddie was now remembering Gemma telling her to think of toddlers when you wanted the men to do something, it made her smile.

Hearing Gemma and Fearghas enter the room from the kitchen, Freddie said. "Tyler dropped these off. He was busy and since he didn't come inside, it was easy to keep the guys hidden. I told him I would give him details later."

She smiled at the men. They smiled back at her. Shaggy large men still wearing towels. She turned to Gemma, waved her hand over the piles or clothes. "I sorted and now they have options until their kilts are dry.

Turning she pointed, "Get in a line."

The men moved and stood for her. But they stood behind one man, Kon-chur? She wanted to remember their names. Well, it was a line, just not the one Freddie had been thinking of. Gemma said that they were quite literal.

Even Gemma giggled.

The girls moved, picked up the sets next to the names and handed them out. The guys took them and held them.

Gemma said, "OK. Now you put them on."

Both women turned beet red and turned quickly when all the towels suddenly dropped.

Gemma nudged Freddie, "think toddlers and believe me, it does work." Both women giggled. Behind them they heard noises, a grunt or two then Gemma was touched on her shoulder.

"They are changed." Fearghas said softly.

He had stayed beside Gemma when she had turned suddenly as his brothers dropped their towels. It was a proper female that he was going to court, he liked that. Not one that ogled a man as a bar wench would. A proper female.

The women turned slowly and saw that indeed, the men were dressed. And correctly it looked. The pants had drawstrings, in the front. A few pants hanging low on slim hips, then there were the shirts....

The shirts that barely covered the wide chests. Strong arms hung out, biceps bulged and they heard a few sleeves tear and Gemma heard her friend inhale.... And turned to see Kon-chur jerk and get his head through now pulling the bottom that went down - to the middle of his chest.

"These guys are not toddlers Gemma." Freddie said with a sigh as she again admired those biceps that she had measured earlier. Yuppers. Biceps. Big guns as her daddy called them.

Sure she had seen arms. Seen chests. She lived on a working ranch before getting her own small spread. But her llama's she could handle with little or no help. Except around shearing time twice a year.

Gemma only nodded. Then she noticed the BVDs now lying on the floor. OK, they don't do underwear? At all? Huh. Or maybe they did not understand the premise of the BVDs first, pants second? How would she explain to them.

You know or this is where a man came in to explain BVDs to someone who didn't.... Nope, not going there.

Gemma caught Freddie looking at her phone. Seeing line after line of texts. She swallowed, "I am having the SuperBowl party here aren't I?"

"Yuppers." was all Freddie said as her thumbs flew sending out another text.

"Well shit." Gemma said and looked at the floor, the guys and now at the clock on the wall she saw it was 1 PM. "I need to get those goodies thawed anyway, might as well start now."

"And I need to run home and get my stuff." Freddie said.

Then both stopped speaking and looking at their phones when Fearghas bent over, now totally nude to pick up a pair of sweatpants.

He frowned as he stood and turned them forward and backward, looked at the men beside him then bent and put his strong, muscled leg in....

Gemma's mind went blank. Looking at the strong thighs, tight ass.....

Freddie's mouth hung open.

Then she turned her back to the man, twisted Gemma along with her and said with a squeak, "I will call if I need anything." and she was out the door throwing her coat on as she moved to jump into her vehicle.

Gemma snapped out of her trance once the man was covered and now standing in front of her and he snapped his fingers under her nose. A huge grin on his face as he watched her go from pink to dark red.

Gemma took a very deep breath and said, "OK. We need to make the best of this situation. First there are a few things I need to show you. Then we need to clean up and get on food patrol."

She gave a swallow seeing the tight T-shirt now covering Fearghas's chest and saw that it did not come all the way down to the waistband of his pants so she now had a view of his lower abs.

The guys looked at her.

She knew she had their attention mentioning food.

And now that they were more covered.....

She cleared her throat, "I have two hours to get set-up.

"It is a party.

At my house, here.

A Super Bowl party not one with music and dancing. Well, there will be music, and dancing for half-time.... Anyway."

She inhaled. Do they understand games, football or?

Chapter 20

Gemma now pointed at each of them like a drill sargent, "This is all new to you. But I have rules. #1 no weapons. I am parking those suckers somewhere safe from your hands and others hands. OK?"

Good, not one attacked her or grunted. For some reason Gemma seemed to understand the grunts. 1 point for her team.

"#2. These are all **my** friends and will be coming here inside my lodge and cause you no harm. I will tell them that **you** are **my** friends from out of town and the airport lost your luggage."

She looked at their faces. (Did she just call her home her lodge?)

Getting nothing but a blank face. (Ya, lost them at airport and luggage. They had no concept of an airport. Luggage maybe.)

"You have no other clothes with you, so you now have these."

She pointed at their sweats.

Still nothing. (These guys don't show emotion much.)

Oh well.

"My friends will watch TV. They will yell and they will get excited."

Fearghas nodded now, "We also yell and get excited." The men nodded as they agreed. Ahh, they did hear her and understand, good.

Gemma grinned. "Yes. Good." Even though she had not noticed much excitement.....

She was sure they understood 'party'. She had read history, they had parties. Parties for everything.

"#3 is a thing called TV." Gemma turned and marched from the room. The guys watched her leave, looked at their leader who shrugged and trotted after her. They followed. They knew people, and party but TV? Had they missed something here in her lodge?

Watching Lady Gemma move through another hall, they saw more pictures on the walls. Family? But these were odd, not painted. Then kept going as she opened another door and into yet another room.

This was one they had checked earlier. Saw the fireplace. High beamed ceiling.

Couches, chairs and a mini-bar on one wall. Large windows that looked back over the yard full of snow and a smaller one towards the front where they saw the metal things that people got in and out of. The snow was bright with the sun bouncing off it. The room was well lit.

But she brought them here for a reason.

They would watch and wait.

A large fireplace was in one wall and another had a big dark thing hanging on it. They entered and stood. Watched Lady Gemma who stopped in the middle of the room and turned to them.

Their minds moved and all of them thought that yes, this Lady Gemma was very wealthy. Her lodge was large. The floors were covered and warm. She had benches with covers on them and the big bench was warm. This she called a 'couch'.

Here colorful blankets draped over large chairs and one covered bench.

There were stairs at the first part of this hall that lead up to where they enjoyed the indoor outhouse. Odd, but they were learning to understand how to operate it. It whooshed and water left only to come back clear. Replacing the soiled water.

The other doorways upstairs stayed closed. But from what they have seen so far, she was alone, quite alone. And defenseless. Not one weapon was seen or found on this lower floor and no furs were around. Only the material that was soft and colorful was seen.

This room would be good for furs on the wood floor for warmth as one sat before a fire.

They stayed quiet in thoughts that she was a witch and still safe and yes, this was the future. But if she changed, and moved to hurt one of them, they would fight her. They had not fought witches or fairies, even gremlins, but they had heard talk. And they had one idea, that would be to cover her from her head to her toes. If she could not see them, she could not curse them.

And as time moved, they learned and they felt a warmth towards Lady Gemma. Saw her as kind and knew that her soul was good.

Fearghas was one lucky man. They watched Lady Gemma and him, she was again doing something. Lady Gemma bent and picked up a small black thing from a low table. This was like the black thing that talked back to her.

She watched them, turned, and…..

The men gasped when the dark thing on the wall lit up and showed people talking and moving.

People were stranded inside.

Captured?

"Witch!"

Men moved, backing out of the room. Bumping into each other and the furniture as they moved backwards with their hands out to hide their face.

She had captured prisoners and kept them in the dark box!

Were they going to be next!

Was this why they could not smell another person here?

How had she shrunk them?

Hearts pumped and hands turned into fists. Flight or fight stance. Kon-chur was heading for the stairs to gather swords. And…..

"**No!**" Gemma yelled. Should they give her a chance? Would she need to touch them to capture them and place them inside the thing?

"Not a witch! TV. This is a TV, something that everyone has here. This IS the future. Don't fear it."

Her voice cracked and this was the first time they heard fear come from her.

Her eyes were big as she pleaded with them. Knowing that now, they could or would do something to her if she was indeed a witch or……

Gemma stood there, scared as hell. Looked at Kon-chur knowing where he was heading, but he had stopped. He would give her a chance to explain?

Her eyes now on Fearghas. Pleading for him to trust her and….. She held the channel changer and had only turned on her TV and now, now she feared for her life.

Yes. The thing on the wall showed people but when the guys looked around it when they finally came closer, they found the people had no bodies. Sat at a table and talked, pointed to the wall behind them and there, another box with people….

The men looked, sniffed, leaned and moved but the people stayed inside the dark thing. Not one looked at the men looking at them. Not one was released from the box hanging on the wall. Could they not see outside the box?

"You captured them?" Someone asked.

They watched as the box people never once looked at them.

Gemma slowly shook her head. Softly she said, "No. It is a TV. I can see people who talk. I can change to another and they are called channels." She made the box change. But watched both Fearghas and Kon-chur. Kon-chur stayed on the stairs, not going up or coming back down. Waiting.

Branhubh backed up and hit the wall. Jumped and looked around. Looked up and down and at the others.

Everyone now looked up and waited.

Gemma watched, then asked, "What?"

She looked at Branhubh. "Are you OK?"

He looked at her, "light." It came out a whisper.

"Light?" Gemma repeated.

Kon-chur said, looking at her from where he was now, inside the room with the others. "You touched the wall and the light came on."

Gemma looked at him. Took a breath seeing him with no weapon in his hand, then thought of what he said, she frowned then remembered. "OK, I get it. There is a light switch. I would touch the light switch, not the wall."

She watched them. "Can I show you?" (Which is what she should have said when she picked up the remote from the table.)

Kon-chur nodded, the other guys moved to let her through. But they kept one eye on the 'box people.'

Gemma turned towards the door and pointed, "this is found beside a door, this is connected to electricity here inside my house. Each room has a switch. You move this," she touched it and the overhead lights came on, she touched it again and the lights went off. Watching the guys she moved her hand to another wall and touched it. Nothing happened.

Everyone stayed quiet as they watched her.

Gemma watched them and wondered what the hell was going to happen when everyone else gets here…..

There was no way she could watch all 5 of them all the time.

"I need everyone to relax. You are big and strong and your reactions are first to attack. I understand it. I would be frightened also if it was me. It's not fair that this has been thrown at you since you arrived."

She heard a grunt from someone.

"I know, everything is odd, different and I am putting pressure on you, shoving all these new things and telling you what to do." She looked at them.

Yes, she was giving orders out, a lot of orders.

"I will do my best to keep you safe."

Now they all looked her up and down wondering what her strengths were. What kind of weapons she hid and where.

She put a hand up when she saw them stare at her. "I don't mean that the people coming will hurt you. Like fight you. I mean that even though they are close friends of mine, they will say things that may or may not disturb you."

In her mind she was thinking of finding their swords and knives and hiding them really really well. But they knew other ways to fight, hand-to-hand. She saw their muscles. Remembered the things they had told her. Knew that they could hurt her or her friends if they felt forced or the urge to fight back.

She did not know their *triggers*. An animal may wiggle an ear,, stomp a foot, you would then pay attention and watch their eyes or see if they got stiff. All things before charging. But these guys? Huh.

Gemma was stumped.

She rubbed her forehead and thought, looking out at them she started. Hoping for understanding. If they could understand, she had a chance.

"You crossed a veil in time." she hesitated. Watched them and saw them listening. She was not their king or queen or whatever a high person was, but they were listening.

"I need to go and make sure things are clean upstairs. I will move your things and keep them safe. My visitors will be using that room."

She looked at them, "No one will touch them but me. That is my promise."

She saw them turn to Fearghas. She waited. She had noticed that they confirmed with him for nearly everything. If he decided not to do as she asked, if he said something the only thing left for her to do was she could send them to the barn.

There was nothing else she could do. But she would separate them, and hey, the barns were clean and had places to stay. That is where the vet or workers would stay when needed. A cot or two could be found and there was always the hay….

She blushed thinking of Fearghas looking at the hay then at her….

Not once had she thought of them taking over, and with THAT thought now in her head…..

For her friends, she would boot the asses of these men out of her home. They were strangers in a strange land. But they were also warriors and could inflict pain.

The guys, her friends, would be here and protecting their wives or girlfriends. A lot could go wrong, so very wrong. She held her breath. Knowing that even a Hi-5 could be interpreted wrong. Could be seen as a threat.

Fearghas spoke, "We will be on our good behavior. I promise my brothers will nay harm your friends if they don't try to fight us."

Gemma closed her eyes and remembered Scott and Tyler and visualized them doing their chest bumps.

Yelling at the teams, ok, screaming at the teams.

Oh dear....

"I need to do things, you can help by not breaking anything." She looked at them. She turned off the TV, sat the remote back on the table and moved from the room.

The men now relaxed. They knew that she meant the 'people box'. She did not want them to break it. Actually they could but not one even wanted to touch it and become trapped inside it.

Barra moved to inspect the TV again. Not finding any scent.

Branhubh touched the wall behind him again then moved to where Lady Gemma touched the wall. The 'switch' she called it was now easily seen. He touched it and the lights turned on. He smiled. He could make light. He beamed at the others and flicked the switch several times.

Kon-chur watched them from one side of the room and Fearghas watched them from the other as they stood on each side of the large window. Both with their arms across their chests.

Seeing the men take turns with the light switch or to touch the window glass, huff on it and see it steam. They would look at the chairs, sit on the long bench one and then try a chair or two. But stayed away from the black box on the wall and the small box on the table.

Drostan put his hands together as he sat in an overstuffed big chair and smiled. "I like this future. I am warm, safe and all I need is some brew and a bed." Everyone turned to him and smiled in agreement. He pushed down on the arms and flexed his arms, the chair moved.

Someone yelled.

Gemma ran back in…

Seeing Drostan's face as he was now 'reclined' she broke down laughing. She moved to him and did her best to stop laughing and explain the chair he was in. His face in shock and his arms now in the air. He breathed fast as he waited.

Once the man was back and upright he bounced out and stared at the chair as he moved away.

Gemma gave another laugh as she sat down, demonstrated the chair then put it back up. Explaining how to use your arms and hands for pressure to lower the chair then put pressure on the foot rest to sit back up.

Standing now she moved out of the room, "If you need anything, just ask." Then turned back, "The other furniture does not do that, only the one chair is a recliner."

She moved back down the hall.

The men watched her leave, looked at each other then looked hard at the furniture as if each one would all move.

Trap them. Or...

They again looked at the fireplace and tilted their heads, studying it. They were closer now and it was more light in the room where earlier it was in shadow.

A glass thing, a window? This wall was of stone, they had all run their hands over it and nodded.

Stone.

And a firepit.

This they recognized.

Wood was stacked beside it.

Did not give the impression that it was different.

But that one chair....

Chapter 21

Gemma made a clean sweep of the bathroom. Grabbing boots and things. Used a large sheet from the closet to toss everything in that she was removing. Wrapping another sheet around the leather with *stuff* on them. Ugh. Dropping everything in the center and tying it all in a knot.

Careful with the swords. Well, she bent to pick up one and instantly dropped it. Gads, how much did it weigh? Feargus was again there, beside her and together they made several trips and got things stuffed into the master bedroom where she slept now. She shoved the weapons, now wiped off, (kinda), under the bed and smoothed the dust ruffle. Stepped back and tilted her head. OK.

She smiled up at the man beside her. The main mess was handled. He had looked around her room but never spoke. He noticed everything as his eyes swept the room.

A bed, a comfortable chair, more doors. He moved when she moved, brought he swords in and gently placed them where she pointed. He noticed her floor was covered by a soft rug that covered the whole area. A peek into a room with a partial opened door showed a different floor.

He only did what was needed. Gemma was glad as those swords were huge, sharp and heavy. She stood, took a look around and moved again, now the extra dirty towels she put in the hamper in her bathroom.

Fearghas gave a grunt when she turned on a light and he saw what was inside. Another bathing room. Her own inside her chambers.

Gemma had wrung out the really wet ones and mopped the first bathroom floor quickly. Double checked the toilet paper stash, backed out of the room and turned off the light after replacing the towels and washcloths.

Nodding to Fearghas they both went downstairs. Gemma was satisfied that the bathroom was now ready for the guests who may use it. Her friends knew of the house and all the rooms. They had all visited throughout the years for different things as she had done at their parents homes.

So if the downstairs bathroom was being used, they would come up here.

The clock by her bed showed that she was running late. She decided to get the frozen food out to thaw first before her shower.

<u>And</u> she had to check on the kilts.

Turning she moved and headed back down stairs. Fearghas followed.

Moving along the hall and pulling her hair up, again putting it into a ponytail she moved down the stairs. Hearing the men still in the other room she moved through to the kitchen. Hit the mudroom, pulled out the many kilts, tossed them into the large basket. Dressed again in her large coat and took them outside to hang up. Fearghas watched her from the doorway. Not following her outside.

This would work even if they froze. The material would not dry properly inside if she hung them in the mudroom. She had to use the line and hoped the breeze and sun would do most of the work even with a short day. Any sunshine and breeze would be better than shoving them one by one into the dryer.

This way, they were out of the way. Drying, hopefully a little. And she would have them on the inside lines when everyone left.

The freezer she opened and pulled her wrapped and labeled packages and in another cupboard she got large trays out. Turned and sat them on the table in the nook. Went and got more trays out. She checked the breads as she pulled the foil off or the plastic off. The pies she would keep wrapped for now and heat them later.

Nodding she turned and gathered the big plates that were long enough to sit them out, she sat them also on the smaller table. Gathering napkins, paper towels, plates, she stepped back.

Good.

Mini loaves of bread. Small hand size pies. She smiled proudly at her work.

The dishwasher had the glasses that she washed yesterday that she wanted to use. She had unconsciously grabbed up all those glasses and put them in the washer. And now was glad she did.

The girls would drink wine and the guys would have beer glasses if they wanted. She knew that they had bottles and cans, but if they wanted or if the girls wanted, she had mugs to hold their beer.

She had a strong feeling to gather the mugs and glasses and clean them. Hey, maybe it had been a premonition that she would have the party here. Then why had she not dreamed of men?

Biting her lip she shook her head and kept working. Knowing she never dreamt of men. No one had intrigued her as the man she met this morning with eyes of dark chocolate. Biceps that put others to shame. Strong hand and......

Giving her head a shake she went back to work. Why even think about a man like Fearghas. OK. He said some nice things while in the barn. Made her think, there was a man. A real man who was thinking of her and....

AS if! She blew some hair off her face. Gave her head a shake and took several deep breaths. As if.

Pops was one that liked his beer in a mug. He would like to get beer mugs when he and mom traveled. So several had names imprinted on them.

The rooms glowed in the sunshine, she was happy. Even finding out that everyone was heading her way this afternoon she was still happy. The home would be filled with people, laughter and food.

The place was large enough for everyone and hey, if she was the only place with full power, then why not. OK. There were five excellent reasons not to have her friends here.....

She pulled glass out and wiped them with a towel and smiled as she worked to ensure they looked clean. Again she hummed while she worked and moved around her area. Turning from the dishwasher after closing the door she looked over to see Fearghas quiet, leaning by the doorway watching her.

He watched her.

She could not read what he was thinking.

He looked thoughtful but not too serious.

Gemma stopped moving as he came closer.

"I will watch as my brothers will also watch. We can learn." He was serious. She was so glad that the TV episode was over and she no longer feared that they would come after her.

Inhaling she said, "I know. But there is so much to learn and there is no time before everyone will arrive." She looked around. "The food is there," she pointed at the table. "I need it to still be there when I come back down here after my shower."

She saw him frown. Then he smiled, "Water falling down, we had that."

Seeing him smile. His face softened and she liked that. No, these guys would not harm her or her friends.....

"I checked your kilts, they finally got clean "but need to dry. So you need to wear those." She pointed to his sweats. And talk to your men, your brothers. The other pants, the smaller ones."

He tilted his head.

She moved to the other room and picked up the BVDs. "These you wear under those pants. These are too," she looked at his crotch, the floor, the underwear in her hand, "to keep your, your jinglies safe."

Fearghas looked at her, then down at his crotch that he wiggled, "Keep me bits safe?" His grin was infectious.

She turned really red. He wanted to laugh but did not. She was embarrassed as to calling him and the men out for not wearing the wee pants to protect his *bits*.

"OK, I have to run, I mean, I have to go and shower. You will watch your men and keep them inside? And," she shook the BVDs.

He smiled and nodded.

Gemma came closer and touched his arm. The wide leather band was still around his biceps that showed his rank was now under her soft hands. "I trust you with my house, my lodge."

She did not know another way to explain it to him. But yes, she trusted him.

Her body wanted to stay beside him. She wanted to learn from stories of what he had seen. Old Scotland.

The tails that her grandfather had told with **his** accent. His eyes lively when he would speak of the lush countryside. Of Castles and moors. Of lakes so cold year around from being glacier fed.

She wondered if that was Fearghas Scotland and if he would ever tell her. And she wondered how she could, in this short span of time, have the feelings for this man that she never had before?

He nodded. Felt the warmth of her hand on him and the soft look in her eyes. There was so much to talk about and he needed time. Did he have time on his side? Would he fall asleep tonight and awake back home? Was there still fighting or would he be back before the fighting started.

Would he close his eyes and be ripped back in time?

That thought shook him up. But if he was but one day before the fight, would he still go? Go and take a chance that the portal would be there to save his arse?

Both lose in thoughts they moved.

She turned and moved from the kitchen and went towards the stairs, looking outside she saw Freddie returning and gave a sigh of relief. Someone would be here to watch the guys.

Gemma moved outside to help Freddie unload her car, Fearghas saw it and followed.

They got the stuff out and got it inside, that is when Gemma noticed that Fearghas was only in socks. But she had to move, let

Freddie handle it and knew that there were more clothes plus several pairs of socks still on the couch in the one room.

And later, much later she had to put the guys in the spare rooms. Her mind was a mess, seeing the big men and visualizing the beds....

But later, much later she would handle that.

Gemma showered as fast as she could, dressed in her red jeans and light blue sweater top. She tried her hair up then down. Left it down and smiled as she turned, leaving her room and went downstairs.

She was not one for loading on make-up so a touch of gloss on her lips and a touch of mascara was all she needed.

There was music playing and Freddie was talking to the guys. Gemma stepped quickly into the family room and checked the mini-fridge to ensure it was working.

Several of the guys were now bringing beers and what-not. Hauling coolers between them as they trooped inside and through to the other room. Nodding to the men who stood stoic and watched.

Freddie had cooked both a turkey and a large ham. This has to be sliced for sandwiches. Hogies, breads and other breads now sat along the cupboards.

Lots of finger foods, Gemma's stuff that had been frozen, which she needed to check on. She moved to stand and noticed the Scotch. Would anyone notice if she got sloshed?

Trying to explain 5 strangers, not one was related, but now here. From Scotland, (can't hide that fact), wearing sweatpants. As their Kilts are hanging on the line, winter time, not going to dry anytime soon…..

Relatives? Maybe.

Distant relatives, ya that could work.

But none of the guys resemble each other. Weight lifters? That made Gemma grin. Yes, but no, she was not going to use that. Highland olympics? That may work and you only had to look at them….

She had watched Highland Games with her grandpa several times.

Saw huge men tossing things the size of telephone poles. Saw them balancing on logs in the water. And saw them all wearing kilts. Strong built men.

Fearghas had looked outside when he was in the kitchen as Gemma left and saw the lines full of their clothing. Looking stiff even in the wind blowing. He again wondered how and why this woman was alone.

Odd. No staff helping her, no males aiding her.

No protection.

Alone. So odd in his time.

Laundry. Cleaning. Cooking.

And this friend of hers, also female, comes and goes without a male escort to travel with. The thing that did not have a horse attached. And she was enclosed, the chair she sat in looked so different than what he expected. And the sound this strange box made……

Barra and Drostan have been hovering around this one. Freddie was shooing them all from the food sitting out. She keeps saying 'it's frozen, relax.' Whatever that meant.

It looked like food. They understood frozen. Cold. Had food that one could not chew showed up?. So why was this just sitting there? Was it ruined? Lady Gemma had said, not to touch it. So they would not.

Fearghas knew that the two men were vying for this Lady Freddie's attention. Knowing that she, like Lady Gemma, was alone. No male protector. The two would follow her like puppies if she allowed it, but herself?

She either had not noticed, or did not care.

Not that it hurt the men's feelings. But they were planning something so Fearghas let Kon-chur know to watch them when he couldn't. There was a need to control the *puppies*.

But now smelling the large platters of meat made his mouth water and he was sure that the others found it hard not to grab some of it. The food from this morning was not much and now?

Everyone was hungry again

He watched now as Lady Gemma appeared, he sensed her closeness, another thing that he would question, but later. Why did she have such a 'hold' on him….

She was dressed differently and he liked it.

Women in pants.

But it showed their figures. He was not complaining.

He could see her lean form, it was not difficult. And color.

Colors he found that he liked. Learning that here, all was different and yes, colorful. Women were not afraid of being alone and having a lodge to themselves.

He had caught the men looking and frowning. Later there would be much discussion about today. The difference in 12 hours.....
The day had been eventful. So many things. To learn it all would be good, but Fearghas had no idea of how long they would be staying.
What would they do if another portal opened?
And, would this one take them back to their time or - not?
Would it be inside or outside?
Was this all all trickery?
Or mayhap, a dream?

Now men were entering and bringing things with them. Women followed along with laughter and hugs amongst the females. They talked and moved. Had food and other things.
Fearghas moved and watched from one wall, the lads stationed themselves throughout the lodge and also watched. Lady Gemma had guards now.
Lady Gemma yawned, covering her mouth.
He saw it and remembered that it had been a long day for her also.
The morning, the fog.
Him and his brothers, fighting and ending up here.
Seeing the woman who made his heart beat strong and his body warm as she came down the stairs.

He moved across the room to her again to reassure her, "I will watch the lads. Yes, this is still all strange. It will take time."
He looked down at her, "I don't understand how we came here. We were in battle. A storm. We were getting pushed back more and more. There were flashes of light.
"The light I saw was from here, from you. " He looked into her eyes. The green pulled at him. He added, "I followed and brought my brothers. Where I go, they go." He saw her nod. He wanted to drown in her eyes. But was pulled away from her as the sounds of her friends grew stronger.

If a portal appeared right at this moment, he, Fearghas would not take it. He wanted this. He wanted Lady Gemma and he wanted to learn, be with her. She was becoming more to mean more to him each minute he breathed. He did not understand it but wanted more.

Those green eyes of hers watching him and not once did she look at him or the men in fear as she had earlier. Now, she trusted him once more.

It made him glad. His heart was beating for her.

His hands were on her arms, rubbing them as he talked, "We stepped through and are now here. We can learn if you give us time." He wanted her to understand that he wanted to stay.

"I understand. But today is a bad day and I have people here. Can you control your men when everyone arrives? They will ask questions. They are curious. And with the TV, the game. You will be left out of so many things…."

She looked at the floor. Saw him in his stocking feet like the others. Because seeing his face, so strong, Gemma knew that he had questions that needed answers. And soon. Could she answer them all?

Fearghas sighed, she stepped closer and leaned into him. With all this, she still worried about him and the lads. He wrapped his arms around her and put his chin on her head. He smelled her hair, his chest expanded when he inhaled. She was soft, frail and she trusted him. The Lass had him fully.

"I don't understand why I trust you. There are so many feelings bouncing around inside me." she said with her arms around his sides. She had not *leaned* on anyone other than her parents. Now, after four lonely years she was ready. And not understanding the first thing about matchmaking from the standpoint of a 12th Century man let alone a warrior, she was taking it one step at a time.

"That is good Lass," he said gruffly, "As I have feelings for you also." This was different for him also. This lass was far different than one he had ever met before. He was at a loss on how to talk, if he could touch and now, she had come to him on her own and leaned on him. Spoked words of more than friendship but it felt good.

He bent his head as he moved to lower his head, and kissed her. It was as if they were made for each other, she fit into him and she kissed him back. His heart thumped in his chest. This was right and ….

A cough, they pulled apart, one step back. Kon-chur stood there, "More noise things are coming." His chin pointed towards the front of the house.

Gemma jumped, her face pinked as she looked up at the two men. Well there goes my status, she thought. Maybe everyone thinks I am easy now. She tossed that thought aside, and will go over that one much later as she clapped her hands.

"OK everyone, show time!" She looked at mens blank faces. "I mean, my guests are here, so smile, be nice and don't hurt anyone. Please."

Freddie stood, no longer with her face buried into her phone, smoothed her hands down her jeans and looked at the men, smiled and said, "They would not…" Her eyes blinked as she saw several eyes on her ….

Grinning back at them she turned to Gemma.

Gemma looked at her, "Don't try, and don't even go there…." She gave her friend a look.

Freddie smiled and moved from the table. "OK. I will be good." She moved to go to the mudroom for door duty. Someone had to endure the guys did not leave it wide open.

Fearghas only wanted Gemma back in his arms.…

Freddie moved to the counter, once everyone was inside, got a large knife and began carving up the huge turkey. And with that, she had everyone's attention. Men silently held good thoughts about those two large turkey legs. Would they wrestle for them, toss money? None had anything on them right now.

But seeing the others enter, men and women. Talking and laughing. The thoughts of getting a leg grew slimmer and slimmer.

Chapter 22

People now came through the doorways. Everyone was talking, moving and doing something. The smells grew with each passage and soon a growl or two from a tummy joined in. No one took notice as the sound of greetings passed back and forth.

Scott, Tyler and Ben hauled the beer and coolers though the back, Marcie and Sherrie carried trays that held more food that smelled good, only a few things needed the stove, the others were in large crockpots that were brought inside boxes, they placed them on the counters and plugged them in. Chatting about the weather, or children.

Someone said names and introductions were made to Gemma's guests.

Marcie stared then blushed grabbing a crockpot and plugging it in. Turning her back on the guys, looked at Freddie and rolled her eyes. Her lips made an 'O'. Freddie smiled, not was not the time to talk about the 'guests' of Gemma's Freddie did not think that even today was not a good time and let it go. Every eye roll or whisper, she ignored for Gemma's sake.

The five men listened and did their best to decipher it all. The speech was fast and with so many moving back and forth, it was hard to follow. But the smells kept bringing them back and they looked at the odd pans that now had tails attaching them to the wall. They murmured back and forth but stayed out of others' way.

Talk. Laughter. Bodies moving easily around as if they all knew where they were supposed to be…. Knew this lodge and was familiar with Lady Gemma.

Chips and salsa, cheese of different varieties along with pickles, olives, cut vegetables. Tray upon tray was placed on the counters and tables and Kon-chur along with Ferghaus watched their brothers carefully that no one made a move.

Food guard duty.

Knowing the lads and their appetites, this would not last long.

The smells alone were making all stomachs growl.

Then Freddie pulled other meats from the oven as she called it and not 'fire pit' and began slicing.

The men nearly drooled.

Tyler, Scott and Ben eyed the five when they came through, and carried things back and forth. Tyler had a partial story which explained why the men were dressed as they were.

They noticed the size and each also saw eyes watching each move they made especially when near Gemma or Freddie. Well hugs and all that was what they did, other than the women who hugged and stayed together. Talking outfits or a new recipe.

So seeing stern faces and hearing a growl or two? Made them think twice about *their* behavior.

And since Gemma's *guests* were in *their* stocking feet, the guys took off their shoes also. Which, the girls all noticed and smiled. Another reason was Kon-chur gave them a mean look then looked at their feet. The three quickly removed their shoes or boots. Tucking them into the mud room and returning. And sure enough, someone had a mop to gather the mud or snow.

Gemma had wood floors, old wood floors and now, in stocking feet, the men needed to watch their steps as they found themselves sliding if they moved too fast on the polished wood.

The girls had mentioned before to remove their shoes, and now, the guys just did it. Huh. The women noticed and nodded to each other. And they also noticed the brawny men who stood off to one side and watched everyone else moving back and forth through Gemma's home had been standing in socks.

A few eyebrows went up, but questions were held back as everyone had a job to do. Tables to setup and soon the game would begin. The girls would later question Gemma about her 'guests'.

And they hoped for some answers. And #1 was, who was eligible?

Ben had headed off to the family room and stacked the fireplace as Gemma had asked him to do when he got a minute. He thought it was because he was a fireman, but he also noticed that two of Gemma's 'guests' watched him carefully as they followed him into the room.

Not intimidating, much. But both were larger than he was. And not talkative. After giving them his name and holding out his hand, they finally took it, gave a shake, but stayed silent.

Ben took the wood, stacked it, checked the flu that it was open, put newspaper under it all, stood and reached up to the mantle, and lit it using the long matches. He had learned a few years back that Pops kept the matches behind the small family photo.

Replacing the screen in front and putting the glass off to one side he turned, got a nod from Gemma's male friends when the flames moved and licked the fresh wood. When the fire looked ok, he turned.

Ben smiled. "Not much to it." He then left the room. Konchur looked at the box of matches, noticed their length, pulled one out and sniffed it. Sulfur. Not a stone and flint to be seen.

He nodded to Barra then bent now, looking carefully at the flames, gave a nod and they then positioned themselves in the room to watch as others who entered, dropped something off and left.

They would protect Lady Gemma's lodge. No other warriors were there but them, they would do what was needed. She had no one around when they arrived, so this became their new job. They would become her Clan if she wanted it that way.

The men who had arrived did so with their own females. Not one acted as if he would lord over Lady Gemma. A good thing. If any of these men had an intention of a fight or hurt, the five would handle it and quickly.

It was as if an oath had been made. This woman sheltered them, fed them, clothed them. They would fight for her if need be.

In the kitchen food moved, and plates came out. Those still in the kitchen were told about paper plates by Becky when she saw Fearghas pick up a plate and study it. It would be used for 'munchies' but not for the heavy food.

Branhubh was sure that it would never work as he sniffed it again, wiggled it with both hands and caused it to tear, then sat the flimsy thing down. He raised his eyes and saw that *they* saw but did not say anything. One female picked up the plate and tossed it into a bin.

The girls watched them. And smiled, thinking that it was cute that they did not understand these simple things. Just thought that their families probably never used paper plates and let it go. Thought that if it was an American thing or whatever. They could look it up later. Like 'what countries used paper plates.' Or something similar.

They would talk to Gemma and Freddie later. Wondering what town / country the men were from. And looked over the food and crossed their fingers that there was enough.

Freddie said something and moved the guys out of the kitchen. They, of course, looked back over their shoulders at the food they were leaving behind, as she made the big men move. "We will feed you soon."

And she saw Marcie and Sherrie's brows rise because the men followed orders from Freddie no questions asked. Then again, Freddie was Gemma's bestie.

Kendel and Tom arrived, laughed and nodded to everyone as they removed jackets and were followed by Paul and Christine. Baby pics were shown, oohh's and aahh's from everyone. Becky and John arrived and all were ushered into the other room saying that 'food is following.'

Getting into the big family room they found places to sit or stand as Tyler and Scott manned the bar. Gemma now pushed in a rolling tray table into the room with the snacks. Followed by the cheese platters and chips that now sat at the bar.

Someone had turned on the TV and now the five Scotsmen lined along the wall beside the window watching.

Arms across their large chests. They did not look *relaxed*, nope.

Freddie thought of a rugby game she had seen once and yes, they reminded her of those men. Huge and strong. Also once she had seen a "Highland Festival." Ya, that is what they looked like.

But Had no clue how to get them to relax. Gemma had mentioned the recliner and Freddie saw them watch as Paul sat in it and pulled Christine into his lap. He gave the arms a shove and Christine giggled and slapped his chest. "Hey I don't get to snuggle with you as often with the kids around." She smiled and settled into him.

Fearghas watched. Married and moving to 'cuddle' with all others around? But not anyone said a word or looked upon the couple. Hum, these men treated women differently?

He and the lads would watch and learn these new customs. He had been around wedded couples, remembered looks going back and forth. Hand holding. A stolen kiss maybe. But to hold another in front of people? Nae.

There was another table set up and the crockpots were brought in and placed on it and plugged in to the nearby outlet. Plates were stacked and all was ready. The guys talking about the teams and players. Watching the 'guests' watch them and the TV.

Tyler offered Kon-chur a beer. Tyler looked up at the man, saw his size and his dark looks. Noticed the long hair, the leather band holding it back from his face. Wondered what kind of guys he hung out with. He looked rough, dark eyes that watched everything. Odd, and these were relatives?

Were they all instructors for exercise or something, or were they movie guys? He would ask Gemma later. He thought about the Olympics also and frowned not knowing how to ask the guys and get any answer. How to learn, be polite and not *act* as an officer when doing it.

Kon-chur looked down at the can placed now in his hand.

Tyler had one in his and pulled the tab. Opening it up. Looked back up at the man who did not blink.

Tyler traded cans with him, opened the other one and took a drink.

Kon-chur looked at the can and put it to his mouth. "Cold." He said frowning.

Tyler looked at him, "Man, it's supposed to be cold."

Gemma was right there by his arm, he was surprised he did not jump. "They like it at room temp. Remember pubs and all?"

Tyler held his hand out, "I will get you a room temperature one and put it in a mug, will that work?"

Gemma took a deep breath, Looked up into the dark eyes, "Can he give you a different one Kon-chur?" The big man nodded yes. His dark eyes following Tyler. Then flicked to Fearghas, caught the nod. Looked down at Lady Gemma, he tilted his head.

Gemma quit biting her lip and smiled up at him, "Thanks," she said softly.

Kon-chur now knew which man to watch. This one was more aggressive than the others. He gave the others a signal and they gave a slight nod back.

Tyler moved about the room asking who wanted to drink what and settled back to tend the bar. From there, he had the whole room in front of him. Just the way he liked it. Observing was his job and he was good at it.

He did not know that now, he was the center of attention.

Tyler got some mugs out and opened several cans that were not cold and poured them for the Scottsmen. The men took them, eyed the beer as Tyler explained, "This is not as strong or dark as ale. I have had that on a trip once, but you will still enjoy the flavors."

Tyler moved away, the men then took a sip. Several looked surprised and easily finished theirs. And held the empty mug in their hand. Not asking for another so their minds would stay clear.

It was also noticed that a few women had 'beers' and the others, like Lady Gemma, had a glass's of wine. She was indeed a Lady. This they noticed more and more. Remembering how she fed them and even laughed when one burped. Reminding them of their family, a mother.

This woman who brought them inside. And did not ask questions of their past or raise any thoughts of harming them. Yea, there was the box on the wall. The one where everyone was here and now watching.

Did not others have a box on the wall? Was this unique? As it was, it was something that neither of them had seen before today. And now, several were talking, pointing at it and agreeing with what was going on inside the odd thing.

Now that the men knew that the box would cause no harm, they did not watch it as much as they watched those near them. The women stayed with or near the ones that brought them. Easy to keep them in sight.

Not one male wore a weapon. Not that the lads had not looked. A small sword or even a dagger could be hidden inside a boot. And the men had removed their boots. And when one bent to sit, each of the five looked carefully. Looked for a hidden weapon. But found none.

Again, a nod was passed around. Shoulders relaxed, postures relaxed and the five did their best to enjoy the talk, and soon, hopefully, the food.

Fearghas stayed in the middle between rooms, watching Lady Gemma to see if she got upset. He wanted to stay centered, not in the room and not in the kitchen. Seeing the women move back and forth knowing that his Lady was not doing all the work now but sharing it. Seeing her smile and converse with the other women. Knowing by her mannerisms that she was happy. He was glad that all went well.

A man would assist when their woman asked, but the men stayed in the other room drinking and eating the small objects that was explained as *finger foods*.

This was not much different than what he was used to seeing. Food and friendship being shared. The women taking care of their menfolk. He relaxed sensing that this world was not too different.

He smiled, *his Lady Gemma*. It sounded good to his ears.

He heard her say to someone, "I got up around 2am, so if I poop out on you, leave me be."

Fearghas frowned, *poop out?* What did that mean? He understood the word, but the phrase? He checked her backside. Not understanding her meaning.

He listened in. Moving closer.

Kendal asked, "Why?"

"There was wind I think that rattled the window, you know about the tin roofs. I looked at the clock. It said 2:02 then went out. I got dressed to check the generators and animals.

"Suz-B-Good and Daisy are calving soon, so I went out. The barn thermometer said 41 degrees. And then the fog came."

She looked around, catching herself, "And that is when the guys showed up. Their plane came in early and also lost their luggage....." She looked at Freddie who smiled and said, "That's right. Lost all their luggage." Freddie then shrugged.

Gemma knew that having Freddie confirm things helped her story. And made the reason that five men were here at her house, wearing sweats that everyone could see did not fit them, more convincing.

Tyler spoke, "Well, I am glad that the stuff fit." He did look at the guys who still stood. He winced. Freddie had given him sizes, but he did a hit and grab. Now seeing the men in the clothes…..

Tall bodies, big chests in the tight shirts. And noticed the girls admiring them also. And one was his wife Sherrie. He frowned. Should have gotten bulky and king sized stuff.

Freddie laughed, "I did my best to measure them, but we had no real choices for clothing real quick."

She looked at Tyler and smiled. Did he get small shirts and loose pants on purpose? She had given him the sizes. But, it also depended on what was available. Not many men around here were built like these guys. So, she let it go.

Chapter 23

The TV was on low but everyone watched. Someone said *commercials*. The warriors looked at each other. Not understanding. The main talk was teams, and the men watched.

Teams, they understood that term. Something had happened, men's attention went to the TV box. The box now louder and the guys talking. And they all cheered with their glasses or cans when the *game* started.

The lads now watched both the men and the black box. Interested in seeing the 'box people' running at each other and taking some down to the ground. They 'box people' wore odd armor and no weapons. The shirts were colored and Drostan said, "clan games."

They nodded in agreement. Clans would do this and play. Use force but no weapons other than their bodies. There would be heads butted and maybe an arm or leg broken. But it was all in fun. These men on the *field* inside the box had head armor and used them when butting another.

Understanding that they were watching a game as what they were used to. The game played in a nearby field near a lodge of one of the clans with others. But not to have so many people watching them do it.

Where a clan would surround others. Drinks, of course. Rough play but not many women watching. And a ball of some sort was used.

Here there were men and women sitting or standing in many benches that surrounded the field inside the black box on the wall. At times some faces were clearly seen then faded to a tiny pin. Lines on the ground that looked like grass. Poles at the ends and loud cheers filled the room, also another man's voice when two would appear and talk to each other. And, at times a female would stand talking into a thing they held.

Some wore color, some wore long hair and would stand and talk to the female.

Colorful and so real. The 'box people' were interesting. And when one thought it was getting good, the picture changed and when one grunted a female would look back and say *commercial.*

Whatever that meant.

People around the room watched as the 'box people' stood and talked. Showed food or showed the metal things moving. Huh. *Commercial.* The warriors again looked at each other, not understanding.

Metal things, little people, children. Talking, playing. But never leaving the box.

The men watched.

They had a short talk earlier. If one being came out of the box, they would kill it. Protect Lady Gemma's friends. Their weapons may be up the stairs, but the five warriors were strong and they would fight.

They had strong hands and arms.

Watching that box was hard, tiring. Lights, colors, flickering. The heat from the fireplace. The smell of the foods. Not having any rest since they appeared here. So many sensory things in one day.

The men were sagging, but did their best to stay alert. Alert for Lady Gemma's safety. She had no one other than them.

The beer was ok, not that they liked it as much as ale from home, but it was wet. And the *finger food* as one female called it was ok, well for now. But when there was a *'break in the game'*, the females left to get more food.

This time the meats were brought in. And breads. Watching now as the men and women friends of Gemma's made their food plates, the men moved to get their plates loaded. This was not different than what was seen before until ….

Kon-chur was pulled to the table by a female and was told to eat. She smiled and held a plate, said *load it up.* She had his arm, and when she touched him she made a face to her friends. Smiling and her eyes wide. She felt a well muscled arm. Of course she knew that since the shirts were short sleeved, but she smiled as she moved.

Kon-chur looked to Fearghas who looked to Gemma. Lady Gemma nodded and Kon-chur moved with the lady, soon all the men helped themselves to the meats and breads. Using sturdy plates they got the hotter foods along with the cold.

Learned that the pots with tails kept the food hot. A nice thing.

Fearghas stood off to one side, arms crossed as he watched and frowned.

Here again, it was Lady Gemma's lodge.

She should have been served first.

But she stood aside and smiled at the others.

Spoke softly to them and then she got a plate to serve herself.

The men tucked the information inside to discuss later. There would be quite a lot as the mental list each man had was getting longer and longer. Now they would have to wait until the guests left the lodge.

Vegetables were tried and the men nodded that it was well liked. Some looked familiar.

The sampling of *dip*.

Some liked, others did not. Faces were made. But not one spit out the food. They had seen Lady Gemma use the funny little white thing for her mouth and they repeated that.

Some foods were sweet, some were bland and a few were quite hot. Barra had made a turn to the man with the beer and grabbed a can and drank the whole thing down. His face was red and he wanted to run outside and put his head in the snow. He never had something that heated his mouth so! Drosten had slapped him on the back.

He would remember that tiny piece of meat. It resembled a chicken leg but tiny. Someone said *hot wings*. But now, he hoped to stop sweating. He rolled his eyes as he drank again.

Becky watched them and stood, "There are dips for the crackers, or the chips or for the veggies." She took a carrot and dipped it in one thing, took a bite. Watched as the men watch her and then they would take a slice of green pepper or carrot and check the dips.

She smiled, "Great guys. Just try the different dishes, if you find one you like that will be good." She went back to John and sat down, he looked at her.

"What?" She said to him, "They didn't know what dip went with what. You don't even know which dip is for veggies and which is for chips." She bumped him on his arm.

Kon-chur watched, he knew of jealousy and only nodded back at the man. He was not taking the man's female. She had come to him, touched him and talked to him. He had not made a move to interfere.

The TV box was interesting. The pictures changed from the men on the field to the *commercials*. The tossing of the ball was understood. Pigskin. That term also understood. Although it was a different looking bladder from a pig than what they were used to seeing.

The guests of Lady Gemma's laughed and drank now from both bottles and cans. Barra and Drostan found the cold ale still not tasteful, but Kon-chur now liked it. His attention shifted to a sound.

He watched as Tom, gave his can a squeeze to make it fold, then put it in a basket. Kon-chur looked at the can in his hand, it was empty now and he squeezed. The can popped and folded. Making the sound, heads turned and a few of Gemma's friends gave him a nod.

This was accepted and Kon-chur noted this.

Freddie pointed to something she called *shrimp*. She moved closer with the plate.

This got their attention, they looked at the tiny things. Sniffed and frowned. The smell was not pleasing and the look of the tiny pink thing did not appeal to them.

She laughed, took one, bit it. Said *don't eat the tail*.

And so, of course, they tried. Big fingers moved to hold the tiny thing and put it in their mouth. A few made faces, Freddie was there with paper napkins for them to spit the food into. She shook her head and laughed, "at least you tried it." Then she moved to share the food with the others.

The men watched as the other men shook their heads but the women nodded and took several along with a spoon full of the red stuff held in a cup. Must be a food that was pleasing for females. Another piece of information for later.

Tyler had been watching everyone. Being a cop his instinct was to watch and observe. OK, the men, the *guests* of his friend wore ill fitting clothes. Sweats. Partially it was his fault that he had ran in and grabbed clothing and tossed it into a bag. Five guys. Handled.

Now seeing them. His sensors went up. And when that happened he was usually on to something. A case to be solved or….

Something here was not - quite - right, and now he stood and moved to Gemma, and taking her arm, "We need to talk.…"

Fearghas was beside him instantly but behind Gemma. Acting as if he would tuck her behind him or closer. His eyes darkened as he looked at the hand on Gemma's and back up at his face. Feargus's face was stone.

Tyler was not a little guy but he was not as built as the man now watching him. Tyler's mouth went dry. He was not used to being threatened and this man? Tyler *felt* very threatened.

"Unhand the female." The voice was soft but sturn. Eyes not wavering.

Tyler looked and saw he had Gemma's arm. "I was taking her somewhere we could talk." He nearly choked on the words.

"Unhand the female." Fearghas repeated, not raising his voice.

Tyler was now surrounded by Gemma's *guests*.

Her very large guests.

The ones he figured were rugby players. Like football here.

Freddie got up, ran over and looked up and around, "Guys, guys, **he** is a friend. Tyler here," she now patted Tyler's shoulder, "He is a friend. Safe, really safe."

Her blue eyes huge and looking from one stern face to another. She did her best to get Tyler to release Gemma but he was not budging. Freddie inhaled and exhaled. Did a quick look around and saw that the others were into the game to really notice what was going on over here by the doorway.

Gemma looked at them all and knew that everyone would soon be staring, "Let's talk in the den." Her face was pink. She knew that someone would question all this.

The men, her guests, were different. Everyone could see that. Now everyone moved as a tight group. Some watching Tyler, others watching Fearghas for a signal to take the man down or…..

Fearghas looked again from the hand on Gemma to the man's face. Determined to get him to release Gemma. Tyler did. Only to let Gemma lead everyone to her Pop's office which now was hers.

Entering the office Gemma held the door until Tyler, Freddie, and all the guys entered then she closed the door. Freddie sat on the corner of the desk and crossed her ankles, watching Tyler who now leaned his butt against it beside her. His arms were across his chest.

"I feel like you will be cross-examining me," Gemma said to him. Her voice sounded hurt.

Tyley then ran a hand through his hair, "Fuck, what is going on here? It feels like I am back on the field facing linebackers." He looked around the room at the men beside the wall , standing behind Gemma, then back at her. "Are you safe?"

Fearghas now stood close to Gemma. "She is safe from us, but you and the others, I question that." His voice quiet but of steel. Tyler's eyebrows shot up. Then he winced at that.

"I have been Gemma's friend since school. I would never harm her. I was told that someone needed clothes. That you showed up, in the middle of a storm by the way, and that your clothes…." His eyes got big.

From one corner of the room, the side window looked out over the back. There, the clothes line full of kilts. Kilts on the line and now flapping in the slight wind.

"Are those kilts?" Tyler asked.

"They showed up unannounced. And their stuff needed to be washed." Gemma bit her lip. "Those are their kilts, their clothing."

In her head she repeated, *not lying, not lying. He is my friend first and an officer of the law.*

"They are family, distant relatives. Scotland. The storm, well the storm...."

Freddie stood and looked at Gemma, "Sorry."

She turned now to Tyler, "Swear".

Tyler looked at her then Gemma.

Gemma's face went red, then white.

"What the hell is going on?" Tyler moved to stand.

Freddie moved closer, shoved his shoulder so he went back to the desk, and sharply said, "Swear."

She was angry at him and everyone remembered that Freddie had a bad temper when pissed. "You are either staying here in Gemma's home as a *friend* or leaving as an officer of the law. Choose wisely."

Tyler looked at the guys, one by one. What he saw was very stoic men looking back at him. "They are not soccer nuts or rugby players are they."

Freddie shook her head and put a hand on his shoulder. Her nice manicured long nails dug into his t-shirt as she squeezed his shoulder near his neck. He winced. The nails dug into him.

Again she asked, "Swear."

She watched him. "If you don't, then you walk out of this room and you will leave here. I will take you off my '*friend*' list and never speak to you again. This **is** that important.

"Look at Gemma. You know her. So why don't you trust her? Why are you questioning her friends? If she tells you they are friends of her family, distant relatives, then who are you to question it?

"So you either let it go and go back to the game or leave the house now. And. You will swear never to repeat what happened in this room to anyone." Freddie looked at Tyler.

Tyler looked at Freddie. "I am asking as a friend, but I can see what this looks like and sounds as if I have to question all this, but if this was my home and someone was questioning my guests...."

He felt her hand on him and knew that she had training, hell he was one of the guys that held the classes for the girls to take. She knew where nerve pressure points were. And he felt his arm growing numb.

"I can walk away and watch the game and just have to keep my mouth shut?"

Freddie nodded yes.

Tyler nodded. "I choose the game and getting more food." He looked at Gemma and then the guys. "Sorry. It is my training to question what I don't understand."

He stood, "Are we good?"

Gemma gave him a weak smile and nodded. Tyler moved to hug Gemma but looking at Ferghas' face he chose not to. He looked at everyone, then left the room.

The door closed, Gemma inhaled, and leaned back into the man standing behind her. Now relaxing after this little '*show-down*' that could have gotten nasty. And then there was her BFF.

Now Freddie said smiling, "Well. I take it that my vulcan hand grip did the job." She made a move of blowing on her fingers then swiping her hands together.

Barra nodded as he moved to her, took her hand gently in his and smiled. "I would like your vulcan thing on me."

Everyone laughed. Relieved.

Fearghas put his arms around Gemma and felt her shake slightly. "All worked well. The story is good."

In his mind though, he would keep an eye on Tyler. A nod from Kun-chur and he knew that another set of eyes would help. The two were so close that it was as if they could read each other's minds.

It worked for them several times.

They left the room and found now that others were happy, acting as if nothing had happened. Several guys turned and were explaining the game to them while food was eaten and drinks flowed.

And the part that Gemma was worried about happened when Ben and Scott stood and did a chest bump? It happened.

She held her breath.

What followed was funny when Kon-chur gave a nod to Drostan and now everyone took turns doing it. Furniture was nearly upended when the girls told them all to 'settle down'!

All moved along fine until half-time.

Five men now turned abruptly and faced away from the TV. Which did not work well for them as the glass reflected the TV.

Gemma was getting more bread and chips and when she came back inside the room, seeing her friends singing along with the songs and…..

Men with red cheeks and necks looking away from the dancers.

Backs stiff, arms crossed.

Gemma looked at the TV and back at the guys and knew, dancers.

Holy Crap.

Barely dressed dancers and singers.

Girls wiggling, bumping and…..

Oh double shit.

It would be funny if, well if it was anyone else. But these guys? And now, facing the window, seeing the reflection from the TV on it.

Their heads lowered or their eyes were closed.

Her brave warriors. There was no way she was getting them out of the room without everyone noticing. So she did not laugh. Nope. She stood there and wrung her hands. Waiting.

Freddie was up and dancing, she moved to grab at the guys and - stopped. Looked at them, at Gemma and then the TV. Her jaw dropped and she moved to be between them and the group watching and singing in front of the TV.

Freddie understood one thing, this was not right having nearly naked dancers grinding away on a platform and everyone in the room seemingly enjoying it. She stood and did beat her hand to the beat but did not wiggle.

For some reason she did not want any of the guys to think bad of her. A thought that did make her nearly laugh since she was usually the one at the bar to find guys to dance and drink with.

Dress code in the 12th Century was not even close to what they had witnessed in the hours since they had arrived and now this? Gemma was at a loss. She looked around at the others who only watched the TV, sang and laughed.

Freddie acted as a guard behind them so if they turned around and looked or said something, she was right there to deflect it. But, that didn't happen.

Not one was paying attention to the 'guests' of Gemma's.

Gemma saw Tyler look back once at the men but kept his mouth shut.

Gemma knew that the men were embarrassed to turn around and that they were stuck in the room. She felt for them but crossed her fingers that it would be over soon.

And her mind wandered to how they thought of her, dressed in pants, living alone…..

The half-time was over. Men laughed, excused themselves to do a bathroom run. The girls moved to clear up some stuff and get other foods from the kitchen.

The five Scotsman spoke low amongst themselves.

Soft words. Nods. Looked around at others and back at the TV. Moved, got more food and stood to one side. The side now where they could escape if something embarrassing came up one the screen again. Anywhere to not be trapped away from a door.

The guys and girls sat back down and again cheered for the players. Talked. Drank. Ate.

Gemma ran outside before it got too dark and got the kilts off the line and brought them in. Draped them over the washer and dryer, later she would pull the lines from the wall Pop had put up for her mom.

Mom would hang her and Gemma's bras on them instead of putting them on the outside line. Mom said that the bulls didn't need to see them. Pop would laugh and say, "I don't have to see them either." And wiggle his brows. If someone came up the drive, Gemma had time to grab them all and shove them into the dryer to hide them, but that never had happened.

She used it often for things that could not be hung outside and could not be in the dryer. A nice blouse. A few sweaters. Her one pair of linen pants.

Gemma put the stiff material down and gave a huff. Hoping that they would dry overnight after they were hung inside. She had forgotten how stiff things got in this weather. She nearly had to karate chop the silly things to fold them. Wincing and hoping the material held and did not break. That would have been bad.

Remembering though that the sheets would crackle and make noise but never had one broken from being hung out in the winter weather. Which was not often. Hanging sheets out was good though. Nothing in the store could match that smell of crawling into bed and smelling fresh sheets…..

Turning, she again saw Fearghas watching.

"You always find me." She smiled at him.

He smiled back, "I dinna plan to lose you." His voice sent small tremors through her. It was all he said, but his eyes told her more. That he would follow her and keep her safe. She remembered back in the barn. What he had said, how he made her feel.

To Gemma, that was a new thing. She had seen it between her friends when they married. Saw it in her Mom and Dad's eyes some mornings when they sat and discussed things.

But Gemma never had that *look* directed at her.

And, she liked it. She liked it a lot.

From when they first met. The morning, the fog, the mystery of it all.

This was from the rock that lay dormant in her field?

Or was it something else? Would they stay or disappear like they were never here?

Gemma shook her head. Walked over to the larger than life man whose attention was on her. His eyes like chocolate when he looked at her. His voice soothed her frayed nerves. His eyes calmed her. And when he kissed her, she melted into a pile of goo and loved every single second of it.

With him she felt safe. With him she figured she could handle anything. A partnership consisted of these things.

Looking up at him as she now stopped directly in front of him, she smiled.

He smiled back and wrapped his arms around her.

Chapter 24

The game ended and everyone did their best to clean up. The girls divied up the leftovers, laughed about who liked what the most, and took things out. The crockpots were gathered along with the hot-plates.

The guys got cans and bottles gathered. And other garbage.

Clanking bags and boxes were hauled out to their vehicles.

Gemma looked around and saw Freddie talking to Barra. She held out her hand and flexed it. Her *Vulcan grip*. Barra smiled as he again took her hand, then he kissed it and Freddie blushed.

Freddie turned to Gemma then and said, "Keep the meat. You will be needing it all with this bunch!"

Gemma nodded back, "Thanks."

Gemma looked and saw only two small fruit pies and one small loaf of bread. Whether the others were eaten or taken home was ok with her. She was content that it all ended on a good note.

Now it was only Freddie left and she moved to get her boots and coat. Barra held her coat for her as she put it on, she looked up at him, "Thank you."

He smiled at her. Freddie blushed again. Then gave a quick hug to Gemma and left. Barra starred at the door she left out of. Watched as she got into the metal thing. It made a noise and lights came on. He jumped thinking that it was a flame, but saw that other metal things had lights also.

Gemma leaned against the counter and gave a big yawn. Shook her head and looked at the men now in her kitchen. "Well, I guess it is time to show you where you will be sleeping."

They did not need to look at Fearghas, just turned and followed Lady Gemma as she moved then went up the stairs. This was her lodge. If she would keep them inside with her or send them outside, it was all up to her.

They had seen the hall with the doors but had not 'searched' them and now….

Gemma moved past the bathroom and opened the door across from it turning on the light. "This one has two beds. Twin beds." She looked at the guys and back at the beds and wondered if the guys would even fit. Would the beds even be long enough?

There was a grunt behind her and she took that as an OK.

Moved and opened the door next to this one. "This has a double bed." She also left the light on to show a bed centered under a window. A plaid quilt spread on this one. Gemma remembered that Grandma said it was called 'Log cabin' style. She looked over her shoulder and saw the men looking in.

"OK, there are two more rooms, one is mine and this," she turned to the door across the hall and opened it, "this is the last guest room."

Turning on the light she showed another double bed, this one was covered with a frost blue spread. The room used to be hers. The bookcase off to the side by a desk still had her trophies from raising the bulls and showing them.

Here, Fearghas stepped inside and moved to the bed and looked down, "My brothers will sleep well tonight." He looked back at the men who nodded to him. He would sleep in this room knowing he would be next door to Gemma. He had been with her when she moved the weapons so he knew he was near her door if needed.

Hell he would sleep on the floor next to her bed if she asked.

Gemma smiled then turned, "Do you all want your weapons back now?" By the looks on their faces, the answer was yes. She moved and the men all backed up allowing her space. Gemma walked to the door at the end and opened it, moving inside she again turned on the light.

Now showing a large room with a big bed off to one side. Gemma went to the bed knelt on the floor and brought up the duster surrounding it. Reaching down she dragged one heavy sword out. Now, the others were beside her now knowing what she was doing and getting the rest so she moved back.

The men acted as if they had just got their favorite toys back. But she saw how they touched the weapons with respect. Only touching their own as they moved back, some still on their knees, and held them.

Gemma felt them relax. The tenseness they held earlier, now gone. Knowing that she had kept them safe as she promised. She had also wiped them off before bringing them here. Lost two towels due to sharp cuts, but that was ok. Fearghas had held them for her to do that. No need for the metals to be harmed.

So worth it by the looks on their faces.

And seeing Fearghas looking at her, also holding his weapons, he nodded. She smiled back.

Gemma watched. The men did not put them on, but held them and grunted here and there between them, talked low at times and nodded to each other. She was glad that she gave them their stuff back. Weapons or not, this belonged to them. Other than the clothing they wore when they arrived, these were the only things that was theirs.

Something personal.

It meant something, grounded them.

Of all the things they saw, touched today and stood by.

This was real, this was theirs and she had returned them as she promised.

Fearghas moved to her, "I am glad to hold my own belongings again." He looked down at her then at his sword in one hand. The item was still stained, most likely with blood.

"I understand." Gemma answered. She looked at the big sword and at the others. "I can give you towels so you can clean them." The men looked at her and nodded.

Gemma moved slightly like she was going to leave the room, but she moved to a door beside her and they all saw another bathing room space. She entered and got some short towels and then pointed to the sink, "If you want to, you can use my bathing room and also the other one in the hall."

She had considered all his men, Fearghas smiled at that.

Yes, his Gemma was a fine woman. A queen in his eyes. She brought them into her bower, her private chambers, and allowed them entry. She released their weapons and again offered her lodge to them.

If everyone they encountered in the realm was as kind as she was, this would be a place to put down roots. To stay.

The men moved, but left the room, to them this was her space and they would stay there now after the retrieval of their things. They would assign each man to a room, noting their size and the beds. Two would be in one with a double bed where Fearghas would have one for his own. The shortest ones in the small beds.

Now, finally alone, Fearghas placed his sword and belts on the floor, moved to Gemma and put his hands on her arms, "We, my brothers and also you, have had a long day. First we were in a battle then in a flash, we were here."

He looked down into her face and hoped she would understand, "I am here. I hope to stay. But only if you are agreed." He stared at her, those green eyes looked up at him.

She did not hesitate, "I agree. I would like you and your brothers to stay. The whole thing is mind-boggling. And you are accepting the changes fast," here she smiled. "Not just the bathing room but my friends and my home. I know that it is all odd to you. And there is so much more. When the snow is gone and we can move about, you will feel more freedom.

"I know that you and the others can ride horses. I will look into getting a few more. There is so much for you to see.

"But yes, I want you to stay. I feel a connection to you that…. I have never felt before." She stepped closer. Her hands touched his chest. She felt him inhale. It was as if he had been holding his breath, waiting.

"I think that I will learn much from you and your brothers. I only hope that the rock does not send you back." Here she saw him frown. "I will explain that later but right now…." She went up on tip-toe and with both hands now on his face she brought him closer and kissed him.

Fearghas felt her soft hands on his face, he felt the warmth calm him down. His body moved, bending to lower himself to her and they kissed. He felt her lips on his and felt something else.
    Acceptance.
    Home, and for the first time, love.

The kiss did not last long but long enough. Both understood that whatever it was, they would take it slow. Fearghas stepped back, smiled at her, picked up his weapons then left her room, turning at the door he said softly, "Sleep well my Lady Gemma." Then he stepped out and closed the door.
    Fearghas moved to his room, laid the belt, knives, sword across the desk and inhaled as he slowly turned. He smelled Gemma in this room. Not just today's smell but a smell that said she lived in this room for a long time.
    That meant that her room now had been one her parents used. He smiled. Looked around and moved to the switch on the wall, here he used it for the first time as he had seen the lads do when downstairs.
    The little switch was tiny to his fingers as he brushed it down, and saw the overhead light go off. Seeing the moonlight come through the window he let it stay dark as he removed his clothes, he moved the covers back to lay on the bed.
    He sat, inhaled deeply again then laid back. Her sweet scent entered him.
    Pulling covers around him he rested in the comfort of the soft bed. Knowing that two were across the hall sharing a space and two were in the tiny beds in the next room.
    Yes. This day has been full of things.
    New things.
    Things he had not experienced before.
    New and wondrous things.

Would he and his brothers learn?

Learn to live here among these people?

He would soon know but now? Now he closed his eyes and slept for the first time in several days.......

Remembering green eyes smiling.

Hoping that here he would be when the sun rose again on the morrow.

Chapter 25

Something woke Fearghas up. Sitting he looked around the strange room. Sunlight poured through the windows and he knew that he missed something. Turning his head he saw his weapons and....

A kilt was now draped over the back of the chair. His kilt. Who knew which one was his? Kon-chur. He had to be the one. But to leave him to sleep? And sleep late?

Standing, Fearghas moved to get dressed. Noticing that also his long leather stocking-like boots were there.

The kilt. Softness stroked his skin. Something he was not used to. Awareness filled him. Also the rough cloth of the brassies was gone. Nothing was rough anymore

Something that his Gemma had done.

The last his clothing had been washed was in a stream, was that a week ago?

Again he smiled. Here he had slept a full night's sleep. He was rested and he had a smile on his face. Not an unknown but something from a long time since his last of any relaxation.

He and the lads had raced across counties, through woods and over moors to get to the village where the fighting was. Passing families going the other way, leaving so not to be killed or captured. Leaving their homes and lands to the English shoving their way into Scotland.

The stories of sadness. Of seeing the neighbor tortured then their lodge burnt. It was hard to fathom until they reached the settlement. Following the smoke in the sky and the smell of fear.

Then the fighting. Doing their best to push back the foreigners from their land. It was either the second or third day that he nearly collapsed on the field. So long without food or water or getting a break. Hoping upon hope that the lads survived.

Then the portal.

Here. Here were he and his best friends, the lads who were brothers. The only family he had left. They were here together. Weren't they?

Dressing, placing his belts on him and his weapons in their sheaths he strode to the door and opened it. The question still on his mind. He stepped into the hall. The sounds of his brothers reached his ears.

Laughter? It had been a long time since that sound had hit his ears.

Moving he entered the bathing room and handled his business. Knowing that the sound of the water would be heard. He finished. Entered the hall again and moved down the stairs. Following his nose to the smell of food and sounds of his men, his brothers.

The only family Fearghas had anymore. He now saw them, it was morning and they survived. Stayed. Safe. His throat closed slightly, he swallowed. Knew that they all turned to him seeing that he now was also awake and joining them. He would keep a stiff upper lip, not seem sad. They may not understand that this was because they survived yet another night.

He had been alone when he first found Kon-chur and together they lived and moved to be on the right side of the law. Careful of what Clans were good and which were bad. To stay alive as younglings on their own without a Clans backing.

To be a rogue and wander some turned to the wrong side of the law. Fearghas was young, but smart. He had learned well and trusted his instincts many many times. And moving with Kon-chur, they did well and survived.

Years passed as the two grew stronger and more wise to the changing world around them. Learning to fight, to live and find food to survive. When in their last young stages they became a group of 3 and then 5. Stayed together and called each other brother.

Barra and Drostan were true brothers that were alone and willing to go with them. Together they moved, and together they fought for what was right. They were with the Clan of Donglal when word came of the English crossing the border and the killing and thieving of young boys and women.

Donglal knew of Fearghas and his strength behind his sword, and the clan of his da had been broken apart. So several traveled together. Moving ahead of the larger Clan, arriving first and finding that the fighting was rampant and sad to hear that they were more than outnumbered.

When they got there, the rains started. They fought hard and shoved the English back twice, then word came from the North where another band of English had entered.

The five again moved as one.

Here they gathered. Ate some leftover rations, drank water and fought for three days when …….

When they were transported here.

Tossed into another world. One where they saw things that were only witchcraft or….. Or truly was the future.

So it was no wonder that they had slept late. Days of no rest. Days of no food. Now, here at this lodge, when Fearghas entered, hearing his brother's soft talk or a laugh, his heart warmed.

They were all safe and well.

Gemma had gotten up at 5am as usual. Dressed and left the house to get to the barns. Keeping her tradition / habit of handling the cattle first then the horses. Making sure that they were all handled then was back inside.

She had checked the kilts that she had hung on the inside lines. Satisfied that they were dry she folded them. Surprised again at their lengths. Holding them she entered the kitchen and - promptly dropped them all.

Surprised.

A big naked man stood there.

Kon-chur had awoken, moved downstairs to find his belongings remembering that Lady Gemma had put them on a line inside, now he stopped, his head tilted in question when he saw what she held. Then frowned when she dropped it all. He bent and picked them up, gave a grunt and turned. Sitting them all on the counter.

He took one, this was more green, he gave it a hard shake that made it *snap* and wrapped himself in it and took the end and, with a toss over his shoulder. He turned back as he gave something a twist. Securing it.

Gemma's face was red.

Well not that often was she confronted by a huge man. OK, this had been a first. And also a first was a naked huge man. In her kitchen. But now he was dressed and softly spoke to her, "My thanks Lady Gemma, the cloth is soft once more, tis like new."

He then moved to retrieve the others.

Gemma noticed then that the kilt was just past his knees. Which was good because when he moved quick....

She looked up at the ceiling, found her voice and asked, "Did you sleep well?"

"Yes mistress, well indeed. The bed up yon is soft like skin. I slept well." He gave her a slow smile. "I will take these to the lads. They will be awaking soon."

Gemma nodded and watched Kon-chur leave. Now covered although bare footed. He must sleep naked. Good Lord now she was thinking of all of them sleeping naked. And she smiled because the man stood there, relaxed, his hair tousled from sleep. He kinda looked cute.....

And also glad that all the men had not been standing there - in the nude.

They slept naked. OK.

Her face pinked again.

Turning in a full circle, finding she was in the kitchen she concentrated on getting food for her *guests*.

Later while all had coffees and Gemma was tossing pancakes as fast as she could make them to the awaiting plates as the men lined her counter. This counter was surrounding the cooking area. And now it was full of big men who were devouring her pancakes faster than she could cook them.

Her mom had designed this kitchen. Pop did the changes during a time she stayed with her sister. When returning she was so surprised. Gemma had been 13 then and remembered helping Pop as much as she could.

Mom loved cooking and facing her family as they ate. This cooktop was gas burners that you could cover with a large plate. Perfect for a pancake breakfast.

Gemma laughed at one face dripping with syrup and then joked with another. Finding that orange juice was not a big hit but milk with the sausages were.

The tube sausage disappeared and she wondered if there was more in the freezer when she looked up and saw Fearghas come down the stairs.

He was fully dressed and also wearing his weapons.

A true warrior.

She opened her eyes wide seeing him advance across the room to her. Their eyes met and she stopped, a spatula in the air and froze. The smell of something getting hot caught her attention and she moved to flip several pancakes…..

Knowing her face was red.

The others moved to make room for the man, their leader. Who now sat directly in front of her as she handled the griddle. Flipping food and moving the sausages cooking there. She remembered that she was thinking of something when he appeared but for the life of her all she knew was that he was awake and sitting in front of her.

Looking so fine in his kilt.

Fearghas smiled, held up a plate. Gemma placed several pancakes on it and then gave him sausage. He smiled at her and gave her a wink, she again blushed. "I canna not believe I ovr-slept." His accent was heavy as he spoke.

"I guess you needed it." Gemma said then bit her lip. "Sorry, I should not make assumptions."

Someone moved a coffee cup to his one side. Another moved the syrup. Fearghas looked down. Looked at the syrup container.

"The cover for the wee flat cakes." Drostan said. "Tis good." His eyes sparkled.

Fearghas looked at the other plates then poured syrup on his. Forking a chunk, he lifted it and put it in his mouth. Sweetness filled his senses. He groaned.

Someone shouldered him.

Everyone laughed.

"Good, Ya?" he heard.

Fearghas nodded and took some more. The coffee was hot and dark. Everything was good. He had not had 'flat cake' before.

New and interesting.

The best part was that he awoke here and not in a field of dead or nearly dead men. Or in a strange place. Remembering that he was naked when he laid down, it was a mistake that he would ner do again. And this was another thing to be discussed.

He crossed his fingers and gave a small prayer that this would hold true and that he and his brothers would be able to stay here.

The morning was over.

The food eaten.

All were in good moods, dressed again in their own clothing they stood and stretched.

Gemma moved as she cleaned her lodge. Humming as she worked.

Again Fearghas wondered when other workers would arrive. Was it that she let them go for a holiday he had no knowledge of?

The ones that were here late yesterday, they did not speak of staff or helpers. They acted as if this was normal. Normal for a female to be living alone.

The small black thing. The object that Gemma talked into. It made a noise. This sound was different reminding him of a bell and Gemma was alerted. Her face turned serious and this made Fearghas alert.

She moved and shoved her feet into boots, tossed her coat on and ran for the other lodge.

"I'm coming!" She yelled.

Now, the men moved to follow her. Bringing their weapons with them. It was unknown what had made Lady Gemma react as she did. And her face, it told them that she was worried.

Gemma was found inside the nearby lodge. Now all the men knew what was here and the size of all the animals inside. They slid to a halt upon entering and kept an eye on the bulls.

And the bulls took notice of them. One snorted and another pawed the ground. Not one left his pen as the big heads swivled to watch Gemma fly past and seeing the men not follow.

It was as if there was a line on the floor. If the men did not pass it, the bulls allowed them to stay.

The men entered and saw all the huge animals. But they did not relax. Something had upset their Gemma and they would not stop until they found it.

Fanning out they moved. Checking high and low to find the problem…..

Hearing a bellow ….

Finding that it came from deeper inside.

Gemma knew what the alarm was since she had a signal attached to the pregnant female's collars. If they were distressed, or in labor, it sent an alarm to her phone.

It was something that was new and in its trial stages. She had heard about it and asked to be included. Stating that she lived alone, had pregnant Brahma's and got the grant.

Gemma was inside one of the pens. "It's ok. It's your baby. Breathe with me." In her hand was her black thing.

She spoke in it. "I will NOT raise my voice for you. You can turn up the volume on your end! She is in labor and <u>you will</u> get out here. Remember, this is her first and I want things to go….

"I don't care where you are. It is monday. If you have a hangover then go vomit then get your ass over here!"

Gemma looked at her phone, "Men!"

Then she stroked the huge head. "It is fine. I am here and we will get you through this." The big female brahma put her head up and bellowed again. Her sides heaved from the contraction. Her eyes wide, showing pain and fear.

Gemma moved to her side, she had already removed her coat. "Come on. Work with me."

She looked up. "Any of you know how to help with a birth?"

Faces of huge brave warriors looked at her, the brahma and back to her.

"Lovely, just lovely." She rubbed the side of the mama bull. "I have a vet who partied too much yesterday and may or may not make it out here let alone make it in time to do any good." She stroked the huge animal's side.

"This is her first. I thought that there would be help…." Her voice drifted off.

"Do we boil water? Lay down cloths? Do you need strong arms?"

Gemma looked up. Saw the men. Closer now. But also keeping an eye on the big bulls that were watching them.

"I need all that. From what I know is that we need to find if the calf is in the right position."

Now the men all looked at each other.

"I can do that part." Gemma smiled at them. "But one of you need to come in here and make friends with her real fast. Because you will need to hold her head while I check. There is no need for her to put me through a wall because of what I am about to do."

Kon-chur moved. "I work with animals."

"That works for me. Here," Gemma took the huge head, stroking it as she talked soft, "Daisy, this guy is a friend who will help us. You need to be nice." She looked up at Kon-chur.

Saw the man place himself in front of the bull, take a stance, feet apart and then he put his hands on her head, one on each side, then lean, touching his forehead to hers.

Gemma watched as the bull's sides rippled again with another contraction. The bull seemed to relax. Her neck muscles did not jerk.

Gemma moved to get behind her. Praying not to get kicked. Pulling the long plastic sleeve up her arm to her shoulder, she looked back around and saw the man keep his head on Daisy's.

Getting into position, standing on a stool, Gemma winced, grunted as she shoved her hand and arm into the bull. Finding hoves and a face she grinned and softly patted Daisy's huge rump as she pulled back out and stepped down.

"The calf is in the right position," she said. Still grinning. Now removing the sleeve and discarding it, she again moved. "We need to keep her resting and work through the contractions. She can't lay down."

Looking up at the man she touched his arm, "Thank you."

The big man kept his hands on the huge head and still stayed forehead to forehead with the bull. Gemma saw the connection and let him do his thing. The wait was not long and the big bull grunted a few times and expelled her calf.

Gemma moved. Daisy shifted and now both worked to clean her baby. Gemma had already pulled the mucus off the calf's mouth and nose and hearing it bleat, leaving the rest for the mama.

Stepping back, leaning against the wood of the stall, she looked on with wonder at the pure white calf then saw the single black ear as it wiggled. Cute. Her eyes teared up. She loved the newborns.

Daisy was doing as she felt, something that was inbred. Cleaning her baby who now stood on his shaking legs, moved to find milk.

Gemma felt strong arms holding her close as she and the others watched the two. Then Gemma moved and got a chart off the wall. Putting down the date and time. She looked at Kon-chur.

"Would you take the honor of naming him?"

The big man looked at her and back at the calf. Nodding and said, "No War."

She blinked at him. "No-War. I like that. OK, that is his name. No-War." Gemma put it on the chart.

She saw the way Kon-chur looked at her then back at the calf. He smiled. The man's face transformed when he smiled. She liked that. And hoped that soon all the men would find something to smile about. To bring them joy, peace.

The sound of gravel and a motor had the men tense up again. Gemma moved to the door and looked out. "It's my vet. You will let him in, he needs to inspect Daisy and the baby." The men nodded and backed away but not far.

They had all been surrounding the pen and watched as their brother did his *magic* on the huge bull. Now, they blended into the background as a man entered with a large case.

"Oh, she had him. Sorry to be late." He looked at Gemma then quickly at the man behind her and at the rather larger one inside with Daisy and the calf. Daisy let out another bellow.

"I said I was sorry." He said to the mama bull as he moved.

Gemma laughed.

Kon-chur stood aside but watched the man handle the new calf. Then as he checked the new mama.

Everything was right. The baby was here and the mother was fine. She could relax until the next birth.

Fearghas looked at his Gemma. New respect. The woman was gentle. Bright. Cheerful. Blushed easily. But when it came to getting things done, she moved in and did it.

She handled her lodge.

She handled meeting fierce warriors.

She cooked, cleaned and now, she assisted in birthing.

He was amazed and proud.

Looking back at his men who were there and saw her as he did, his chest widened. Crossing his arms he watched the man whom Gemma allowed near her Daisy.

The man was a medicine man from what Fearghas could see. Carrying things in his bag. Now handling the after-birth as it was expelled.

Checking the new calf. Confirming with Gemma. Making notes.

Fearghas watched. Stayed patient and watchful.

A man who came at Gemma's bidding.

Who is this woman?

Chapter 26

Gemma had no idea of what was going through the men's minds as they watched everything closely. Standing tall, arms crossed. She was surprised that the Vet had not turned around and jump back into his truck seeing the men there.

Kilts. Weapons. Weapons? She looked up sharply and yup, they were all armed to the teeth and not one was smiling. They watched the Vet.

Holy Crap. She will have some explaining to do.

But her Vet was doing his job. Examining Daisy and the calf, not paying any attention to the men there as if it was an everyday thing of Gemma having a man here let alone 5.

Then she thought of yesterday and also the towns 'voice telegraph'. Ya. She bet that everyone now knows of her 'cousins'. OK. So much for keeping the guys on the down-low.

She could not let that distract her now. It was Daisy and her newborn that was important and nothing else. She was here, the vet was here. What people were saying in town was nothing that she could control.

Gemma watched the Vet. He did his job and they compared notes. Holding her chart on the clipboard, Gemma explained that she checked to find the calf before the birth. He nodded. Made his own notes.

Picked up the afterbirth and bagged it for her. They would get the weight and measurements later. No need to get between a new mother and her baby. And there was always a weight difference from birth to a three day old. He said he would return on Thursday or Friday to follow through.

All went fine, he gave her a nod. Turned to Daisy and praised her and said 'she did an excellent job for the birth', before he turned and left. Again not paying attention to the men as he passed them.

Gemma wondered about that but knew that he had seen them and would make his own 'addition' to the story floating around. It was a small town and yes, others would be talking about her and the men that several had seen here at her Super Bowl party.

Gemma moved back to Daisy, gave her extra food and doubled the water. Watched the two as they bonded. The calf flicked his ears as he nursed. Seeing his pink skin, the two ears, one solid black. She looked over at Come-N-GetMe and gave him a thumbs up.

Cotton Candy had stayed pinkish than a light tan but this one may be white. His mama was white and black in the legs.

All was well in the animal kingdom. Gemma leaned against the railing and sighed. The hard part was over. Daisy and her calf passed all tests and now, watching the little guy suckle making slurpy noises, filled her heart.

This is what she was. A rancher. One with a breed of cattle that others found discouraging and frightful. The stories of bulls being goaded and forced, even at rodeos. Gemma kept her stock away from them. Imagine if they talked and had a bull mutiny? She gave a snort, turned and checked on Suz-B-Good.

As the bull nudged Gemma who cooed to her. Then saying, "you are next. Try to give me a day or two ok?" Gemma looked at the newborn and at Suz-B-Good and wondered what color her calf would be?

Now turning and moving, she was ready to leave the barn.

Looking around, seeing the men but noticing that they were more relaxed now. Glad that things were going well she moved to pass them. No more surprises and Gemma was 'coming down' from the high earlier.

The complexity of a birth would do that. So many things could go wrong. But, all is good and now Gemma could again relax. Noticing that Fearghas stayed beside her as she moved across the drive, up the wide porch and entered the house. She was worn out, even if the work was all done by Daisy, there was a lot of adrenaline flow there.

Moving along and knowing that the men moved with her was. Huh. Like her own team or group. Nice. She knew that they would not harm her and here, they were safe for now.

Not even was she going to think that in a blink, they could be gone. But they had woken this morning, here and still in one piece. Naked but in one piece. Her face pinked, naked. Why in the hell did she have to think of that?

Nice. And she would worry about what was said in town later. Right now? She needed to make some notifications in the office of the birth, but now? A celebratory drink was in order.

One of Pops traditions. They always had a drink with a birth.

His Queen. She handled everything that came up. She did not need weapons, she used her brain. Watching how she handled things and made the man do her bidding. Seeing her gentleness with the animals.

Remembering how she handled a lodge full of people and foods. There had only been one mishap, when the one man took her arm. And a smile crossed Fearghas's face remembering how fierce Lady Freddie got.

Now, allowing Kon-chur to name the calf. That was something not necessary. But Kon-chur had indeed calmed the mother. And Fearghas saw his brother's reaction to naming the calf.

The little guy was all pink and would soon be white, other than one ear. Solid black. And in naming it, Kon-chur had a connection. A solid connection to the here and now. Would this be all that was needed to keep them here?

Fearghas hoped.

He had seen Gemma look over at the one large bull towards the back. He was all black. Mean looking. Were these all his herd? And now, looking around he saw that yes, they had been either mated or sired by the big bull.

Strength was there. The bull was indeed strong.

When she hummed, all the animals calmed down. She cleaned and made sure they all had food and water before leaving. Yes, her babies as Lady Freddie had said.

Fearghas was proud to be near her. His Queen. And knew that Lady Gemma would make an excellent mother one day.

A metal thing came up the drive. Barra moved to go to it as he recognized the metal thing, before it stopped. Recognizing it from yesterday.

Freddie got out and waved. Going to the next door she opened it and started pulling out bags. Barra helped. They moved to the house.

Freddie was happy, she had hit the stores early and picked up a few things. She pulled out coats and checked a slip in her hand to hand them out. She had taken the measurements and had the sizes and personally handled it this time.

The men had never had a covering other than a blanket or furs to drape over their shoulders. These were new to them. Something with sleeves and now, they held them and looked at each other. A large shirt, they could do this.

Freddie put her hands on her hips. "Well, if you removed a sword or two, they just may fit." And she waited. They looked at her, looked at the coats and moved to remove the huge swords across their backs.

Gemma smiled, watched and waited. These guys could fight, kill and here a blonde woman was giving them orders.

The men watched each other as they put the coat on. After seeing Gemma do it several times of course they were familiar Finding that it was not that bad. And after some wiggling, they were content to keep their chests warm when outside.

Freddie gave a sigh. Now those chests were covered and she is the one that caused it. Then soon, because they were inside, they removed the coats and walked them to the hooks in the mud room.

Gemma could have clapped her hands together. She was so proud of them and knew that they had been watching <u>everything</u> she did. Studying her and her actions. Things were looking up.

Freddie was just happy to see the chests bared again.

The men entered, moved through the room that he heard Gemma call 'mudroom'. Though they had looked and not seen the mud. Continuing on they watched her as she moved to a cupboard and removed a bottle, turned to another and grabbed tiny glasses and plopped them on the counter that resembled a bar with a hot thing Gemma cooked on in the middle.

She called it a 'cooktop' and he remembered the flat cakes from earlier.

Gemma put 7 glasses down, and opened the bottle and poured.

"My Pop would have a drink to Christen the newborn. I would like you to share this with me." She looked at them all, then grabbed a glass and held it up.

The men followed and Gemma said, "To No-War."

They smiled, "To No-War".

All clinked glasses and drank the shots down. Freddie winked as she sat the shot glass down. "I guess I arrived in time. Do we have a boy or a girl?"

"Male," Kon-chur added. Then he ducked his head for speaking out. No one said anything. He felt better and would remember that he was no longer home.

The men were slightly surprised at the taste, it was of home and family. Memories of having a drink for a birth or of a fight or a good hunt, went through them. The whiskey was good and they at first, sipped but now, drank it down with gusto. Glad to be alive and enjoy a new tradition in this future.

Fearghas was beside Gemma later and he watched her, saw her do some cleaning and started on lunch. He stepped closer and put his hand on her shoulder to stop her. Gemma looked up at him.

"I canna understand this." He waved one hand. "You work, you do all the work. You don't have a lad to help or a woman to help ye . I see you clean and cook. I see you with your cattle. I see you with your friends."

He looked at those green eyes that looked up at him. "I ner met a Lass like you. Alone and," he looked up as if he had to choose his words. "I thought you a witch." He felt her tense.

"I learned, ye are not. This year 2015 is difficult to yet understand. I will need to learn much if I and me brothers stay."

Gemma smiled. "I am relieved that you know I am not a witch. Scared the hell out of me when I first heard it." She looked down. Blushed, "I want you to stay." Looking up she waited, watched the face that she had seen go from stone hard as when he arrived, then to wonder as he saw different things and showed confusion. Then to being happy.

Right now his face was soft and she felt his large hand on her cheek. His thumb stroking her beside her ear.

"Please stay. Stay here and learn. We can work out what is needed and go over things again and again when you don't understand. I like your brothers but," she blushed bright red.

Fearghas had his palm on her cheek. "I will follow you Lass. Become your warrior if that is what you want. Your protector and do as ye order me. And my brothers will follow me."

Then he bent, touched his lips to hers.

Gemma gave a sigh and went up on tip-toe, her arms moved and circled around his neck.

Fearghas lifted her in his strong arms and they kissed deeply.

Kon-chur was entering the area and saw the two in Gemma's room she called her office. Smiling he turned an about face and left the two alone.

Epilogue

Summer was full of surprises. Getting the men adjusted and introducing them to riding in a tin can. Shopping for 'man wear' and more. Finding it so much easier to handle it on-line. She now had the sizes and soon boxes were dropped off every week until the men had a closet of choices.

Yes, they still woke up in wonder. Knowing that there was always a chance that there would be another portal. Not just for them but to send another through. They stayed vigilant.

When they took their first tour off the ranch they saw homes of color and size. Watched people, seeing other men dressed in pants. Learned to shake hands, nod and smile just a little bit more.

Finding that they could read very little, Gemma had grabbed every book large and small full of pictures of everything. Soon the office became a classroom and a board was set up to hold pictures of what they were learning.

Tractors. Trucks. Cars. Trains. Fairs and groups. Groups of people doing things to show how life here was. Children at desks in classrooms.

The TV became a teaching tool also. PBS was great for that. The men would laugh at the kid shows but they learned and learned quickly. And now, each could sign their name.

Gemma got used to the 'fighting area' that was set up in a corner of the unused pasture. At first the brahmas watched, curious, and now they ignored watching the men spar until they dropped from exhaustion.

It was explained to her that they needed this and Gemma only smiled back. Not often did she say no to either of them. Unless it was a hand going across the table of food.

She shopped around for horses, a surprise for the men. She knew they could ride but with only two animals fit to ride she needed more. Jack, Pop's horse passed and the other older one was kept in the pasture. With only two rideable it was a shame to leave someone behind.

The day the truck pulled in pulling the trailer Gemma grabbed the men and pulled them outside. The truck stopped and Gemma turned to explain. "I understand you like to earn what you have. For you to help me, you will accept what is in the trailer. You will be able to help me here," she waved her hand. "And in doing so, you will earn this gift and call it a transaction."

She looked at them. Saw them look at her, the trailer and when they heard a hoof thunk and a whinny they moved. The trailer opened and they saw the animals. They moved carefully. Murmuring soft words as they touched the horses.

Not just any horses. Gemma had seen their bulk and knew she had to get something that would hold the men. Deciding on what she wanted she had asked Fearghas for permission before jumping in.

He looked at her computer, saw and understood. Smiled and lifted her up in a sweeping motion. "You are the best Queen." Then he sat her on her desk and kissed her until she squeeked.

Gemma after getting her control back made a call to order four Gypsey Vanners. A horse in the draft horse family. Fearghas liked the quarter horse that he rode with Gemma. The bigger horses would work well for the men.

The men mumbled, turned and came out of the trailer. Stopped in front of Gemma and knelt. "We are honored and do accept the gift." Of course, Gemma cried.

They took a trip to Freddies, of course on horseback. and saw the llamas. Another animal they had never seen and watching their reaction was priceless.

There were several small ones and Freddie would clap her hands to get them to run to her. She did her best to follow the guidelines that Gemma had with her animals.

Fearghas stayed close to Gemma. They moved as one when off the ranch. The men still called her Lady Gemma but learned not to when away. Or in groups. They rode when they could and learned to squeeze into a vehicle.

Learning the metal thing but not wholly trusting it.

Gemma and Fearghas had rode out to Stone-Mas after the snows had left. Getting down and standing beside it she talked. The stone was not a small thing but a large boulder sitting alone in the far corner of the field. It was about 4' high and possibly 7' around. The stone held many colors and Gemma pointed to the area where she had chipped the piece off.

She told him of the history and of her Great-grandfather's stories. And cried when she said it vibrated so hard it even spooked the horses when her mother died. Today, she saw that it had another slight crack. This one showed red as it zig-zagged across a corner. She traced it with her finger.

Putting her hand on it she felt the vibration. It was still there, To her this meant that the stone still *lived*.

Fearghas watched Gemma, saw her face and bent. He placed his hand over hers and also felt the rock vibrate. It went up his arm and he turned to her.

They were now nose to nose. They kissed holding the rock with one hand and he had his other on her back, holding her to him. Fearghas felt it. His lightning. He again heard his mother's voice, *love is like lightning. When it is there you have to grab it before it is gone.'*

He looked at the line, the crack. The crack resembled a lightning bolt.

Fearghas kissed her again, this time deeply, they were now in each other's arms.

He wanted to lay her down and love her, but held himself together. He saw her as his and until the time when she told him yes, he would wait.

The
End

Stay tuned, there is more to come. The next book is Freddie's and I need to make a choice. Which brother will she choose? OMG this could be fun. OK, you all know that it will be fun!

So hang in there for : The Stone-Mas (Lightning In The Winter) BK 2 Freddie & _____.

Thought that I would name him didn't ya?

RJ Vlier
Author / Writer

Lightning Source UK Ltd.
Milton Keynes UK
UKHW011013210820
368606UK00001B/74